"Claudia, tell me when you're off duty..."

"Whatever for?"

"Because I shall call for you and we will spend the rest of the day together."

"Oh, will we? Have I been asked?"

"Ah, forgive me, I presumed that you would like to see me again just as I would like to see you."

"Well," exclaimed Claudia, "whatever next...."

"Just so, that is what I wish to find out."

A remark from Mr. Tait-Bullen which needed to be thought about, and still remained puzzling.

Betty Neels spent her childhood and youth in Devonshire, England, before training as a nurse and midwife. She was an army nursing sister during the war, married a Dutchman and subsequently lived in Holland for fourteen years. She lives with her husband in Dorset, and has a daughter and grandson. Her hobbies are reading, animals, old buildings and writing. Betty started to write on retirement from nursing, incited by a lady in a library bemoaning the lack of romantic novels.

Books by Betty Neels

HARLEQUIN ROMANCE®
3583—THE DAUGHTER OF THE MANOR
3601—MATILDA'S WEDDING

Don't miss any of our special offers. Write to us at the following address for information on our newest releases.

Harlequin Reader Service
U.S.: 3010 Walden Ave., P.O. Box 1325, Buffalo, NY 14269
Canadian: P.O. Box 609, Fort Erie, Ont. L2A 5X3

A WINTER
LOVE STORY
Betty Neels

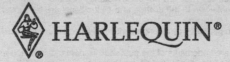

TORONTO • NEW YORK • LONDON
AMSTERDAM • PARIS • SYDNEY • HAMBURG
STOCKHOLM • ATHENS • TOKYO • MILAN • MADRID
PRAGUE • WARSAW • BUDAPEST • AUCKLAND

ISBN 0-373-03626-4

A WINTER LOVE STORY

First North American Publication 2000.

Copyright © 1998 by Betty Neels.

CHAPTER ONE

CLAUDIA leaned up, took another armful of books from the shelves lining the little room, put them on the table beside her and sneezed as a cloud of mummified dust rose from them. What had possessed her, she wondered, to take on the task of dusting her great-uncle William's library when she could have been enjoying these few weeks at home doing as she pleased?

She picked up her duster, sneezed again, and bent to her task, a tall, slim but shapely girl with a lovely face and shining copper hair, which was piled untidily on top of her head and half covered by another duster, secured by a piece of string. Her shapely person was shrouded in a large print pinny several sizes too big, her face had a dusty smear on one cheek and her nose shone. Nevertheless she looked beautiful, and the man watching her from the half-open door smiled his appreciation before giving a little cough.

Claudia looked over her shoulder at him. There was nothing about him to make her feel uneasy—indeed, he was the epitome of understated elegance, with an air of assurance which was in itself reassuring. He was a big man, very tall and powerfully built, not so very young but with the kind of good looks which could only improve with age. His hair was pepper and salt, cut short. He might be in his late thirties. Claudia wondered who he was.

'Have you come to see Great-Uncle William or my mother? You came in through the wrong door—but of course you weren't to know that.' She smiled at him kindly, not wishing him to feel awkward.

He showed no signs of discomfort. 'Colonel Ramsay.' His commanding nose twisted at the dust. 'Should you not open a window? The dust…'

'Oh, they don't open. They're frightfully old—the original ones from when the house was built. Why do you want to see Colonel Ramsay?'

He looked at her before he answered. 'He asked me to call.'

'None of my business?' She clapped two aged tomes together and sent another cloud of dust across the room. 'Go back the way you came,' she told him, 'out of the side door and ring the front doorbell. Tombs will admit you.'

She gave him a nod and turned back to the shelves. Probably someone from Great-Uncle William's solicitor.

'I don't think I like him much,' said Claudia to the silent room. All the same she had to admit that she would have liked to know more about him.

She saw him again, not half an hour later, when, the duster removed from her head and her hands washed, she went along to the kitchen for coffee.

The house was large and rambling, and now, on the edge of winter, with an antiquated heating system, several of its rooms were decidedly chilly. Only the kitchen was cosy, with the Aga warming it, and since there were only her mother, Mrs Pratt the housekeeper, Jennie the maid and, of course, Tombs, who seemed to Claudia to be as old as the house, if not older, it was here that they had their morning coffee.

If there were visitors Mrs Ramsay sat in chilly state in the drawing room and dispensed coffee from a Sèvres coffee pot arranged on a silver tray, but in the kitchen they all had their individual mugs. However, despite this democratic behaviour, no one would have dreamt of sitting down or drinking their coffee until Mrs Ramsay had taken her place at the head of the table and lifted her own special mug to her lips.

Claudia breezed into the kitchen with Rob the Labrador at her heels. Her mother was already there, and sitting beside her, looking as though it was something he had been doing all his life, was the strange man. He got to his feet as she went in, and so did Tombs, and Claudia stopped halfway to the table.

She didn't speak for a moment, but raised eloquent eyebrows at her mother. Mrs Ramsay said comfortably, 'Yes, I know, dear, we ought to be in the drawing room. But there's been a fall of soot so the fire can't be lighted. And Dr Tait-Bullen likes kitchens.'

She smiled round the table, gathering murmured agreements while the doctor looked amused.

'Come and drink your coffee, Claudia,' went on Mrs Ramsay. 'This is Dr Tait-Bullen who came to see Uncle William. My daughter, Claudia.'

Claudia inclined her head, and said, 'How do you do?' in a rather frosty manner. He could have told her, she thought, instead of just walking away as he had done. 'Uncle William isn't ill?' she asked.

The doctor glanced at her mother before replying. 'Colonel Ramsay has a heart condition which I believe may benefit from surgery.'

'He's ill? But Dr Willis saw him last week—he didn't say anything. Are you sure?'

Dr Tait-Bullen, a surgeon of some fame within his profession, assured her gravely that he was sure. 'Dr Willis very wisely said nothing until he had a second opinion.'

'Then why isn't he here now?' demanded Claudia. 'You could be wrong, whatever you say.'

'Of course. Dr Willis was to have met me here this morning, but I understand that a last-minute emergency prevented him. I have been called in as consultant, but the decision concerning the Colonel's further treatment rests with his doctor and himself.' He added gently, 'I was asked my opinion, nothing more.'

Mrs Ramsay cast a look at Claudia. Sometimes a daughter with red hair could be a problem. She said carefully, 'You may depend upon Dr Willis getting the very best advice darling.'

Claudia stared across the table at him, and he met her look with an impassive face. If he was annoyed he showed no sign of it.

'What do you advise?' she asked him.

'Dr Willis will come presently. I think we should wait until he is here. He and I will need to talk.'

'But is Great Uncle William ill? I mean, really ill?'

Her mother interrupted. 'Claudia, we mustn't badger Dr Tait-Bullen.' She looked round the table. 'More coffee for anyone?'

Claudia pushed back her chair. 'No, thank you, Mother. I'll go and get on with the books. Tombs knows where I am if I'm wanted.'

She smiled at the butler and whisked herself out of the room, allowing the smile to embrace everyone there.

Back in the library, she set about clearing the shelves, banging books together in clouds of dust, wielding her duster with quite unnecessary vigour. She had behaved very badly and she was sorry about it—and a bit puzzled too, for she liked him. What had possessed her to be so rude? She had behaved like a self-conscious teenager. She ought to apologise. Tombs, she knew, would come and tell her what was happening from time to time, so when the doctor was about to leave she would say something polite...

She spent a few minutes making up suitable speeches—a dignified apology, brief and matter-of-fact. She tried out several versions, anxious to get it right. She was halfway through her final choice when she was interrupted.

'If those gracious words were meant for me,' said Dr Tait-Bullen, 'I am flattered.'

He was leaning against the door behind her, smiling at her, and she smiled back without meaning to. 'Well, they were. I was rude. I was going to apologise to you before you left.'

'Quite unnecessary, Miss Ramsay. One must make allowances for red hair and unpleasant news.'

'Now you're being rude,' she muttered, but went on anxiously. 'You really meant that? Great Uncle William is seriously ill? I can see no reason why I shouldn't be told. I'm not a child.'

He studied her briefly. 'No, you are not a child, but Dr Willis and I must talk first.' He came into the room, moved a pile of books and sat down on the table. 'This is a delightful house, but surely rather large for the three of you?'

He spoke idly and she answered him readily. 'Well, yes, but it's been in the family for a long time. Most of the rooms are shut up, so it's easy enough to run. Tombs has been here for ever, and Mrs Pratt and Jennie have been here for years and years. The gardens have got a bit out of hand, but old Stokes from the village comes up to help me.'

'You have a job?'

'I did have. Path Lab assistant—not trained, of course,

just general dogsbody. But London's too far off. I've applied for several jobs which aren't so far away so that I can come home often.'

He said casually, 'Ah, yes of course. Salisbury, Southampton, Exeter—they are all within reasonable distance.'

'And there are several private hospitals too. I didn't much like London.' She added chattily, 'Do you live there?'

'Most of my work is done there.'

She supposed that he hadn't added to that because Tombs had joined them.

'Dr Willis has arrived, sir.' He looked at Claudia. 'Mrs Ramsay is in the morning room, Miss Claudia. Jennie has lighted the fire there for the convenience of the doctors.'

'Thank you, Tombs.' She glanced at the doctor. 'You'll want to go with Tombs. I'll come presently—I must just tidy myself.'

Left to herself, she took off her pinny, dragged a comb through her hair and went in search of her mother.

Mrs Ramsay was with the two men, making small talk before they began their discussion of their patient's condition. She was still a strikingly beautiful woman, wearing her fifty years lightly. Her hair, once as bright as her daughter's, was streaked with silver, but she was still slim and graceful. She was listening to something Dr Willis was saying, smiling up at him, her hand on his coat-sleeve. They were old friends; he had treated her husband before his death several years ago, and since he was a widower, living in a rather gloomy house in the village with an equally gloomy elderly housekeeper, he was a frequent visitor at the Ramsays' house.

He looked up as Claudia joined them.

'My dear, there you are. Come to keep your mother company for a while? Are we to stay here, or would you prefer us to go to the study?'

'No, no, stay here. There's a fire specially lighted for you. Claudia and I will go and see to lunch.' She paused at the door. 'You will tell us exactly what is wrong?'

'Of course.'

In the dining room, helping her mother to set the lunch, Claudia asked, 'Is Great-Uncle William really very ill, Mother?'

'Well, dear, I'm afraid so. He hasn't really been very well for some time, but we couldn't persuade him to have a second opinion. This Dr Tait-Bullen seems a nice man.'

'Nice?' Claudia hesitated. 'Yes, I'm sure he is.' 'Nice,' she reflected, hardly described him; it was far too anaemic a word. Beneath the professional polite detachment she suspected there was a man she would very much like to know.

They were standing idly at the windows, looking out into the wintry garden, when Tombs came to tell them that the doctors had come downstairs from seeing their patient.

Dr Willis went straight to Mrs Ramsay and took her hand. He was a tall, thin man, with a craggy face softened by a comforting smile as he looked at her. He didn't say anything. Claudia saw her mother return his look and swallowed a sudden surprised breath. The look had been one of trust and affection. Don't beat about the bush, Claudia admonished herself silently. They're in love.

There was no chance to think about it; Dr Tait-Bullen was speaking. Great Uncle William needed a triple bypass, and without undue loss of time. The one difficulty, he pointed out, was that the patient had no intention of agreeing to an operation.

Claudia asked quickly, 'Would that cure him? Would he be able to lead a normal life—be up and about again?'

'The Colonel is an old man, but he should be able to live the life of a man of his age.'

'Yes, but...'

'Claudia, let Dr Tait-Bullen finish...'

'Sorry.' She flushed and he watched the colour creep into her cheeks before he said, 'I quite understand your anxiety. If Dr Willis wishes, I will come again very shortly and do my best to change the Colonel's mind. I feel sure that if anyone can do that it will be he, for they have known each other for a long time. I can but advise.'

He glanced at the other man. 'We have discussed what is best to be done—there are certain drugs which will help, diet, suitable physiotherapy...'

'I'm sure you have done everything within your power, Doctor,' said Mrs Ramsay. 'We will do our best to persuade Uncle William, and if you would keep an eye on him?' She looked at Dr Willis. 'That is, if you don't mind, George?'

'I am only too glad of expert advice.'

'Oh, good. You'll stay for lunch, Dr Tait-Bullen? In half an hour or so...'

'I must return to London, Mrs Ramsay. You will forgive me if I refuse your kind invitation.'

He shook hands with her, and then with Dr Willis. 'We will be in touch.'

'Claudia, take Dr Tait-Bullen to his car, will you, dear?'

They walked through the house together, out of the door and across the neglected sweep of gravel to where a dark grey Rolls Royce stood. Claudia stared at it reflectively.

'Are you just a doctor?' she wanted to know. 'Or someone more important?' She glanced at his quiet face. 'Mother called you Doctor, so I thought you were. You're not, are you?'

'Indeed, I am a doctor. I am also a surgeon…'

'So you're *Mr* Tait-Bullen. You're not a professor or anything like that, are you?'

'I'm afraid so…'

'You might have said so.'

'Quite unnecessary. Besides, being called a professor makes me feel old.'

'You're not old.'

He answered her without rancour. 'Thirty-nine. And you?'

She had asked for that. Anyway, what did it matter? 'I'm very nearly twenty-seven,' she told him.

He said smoothly, 'I am surprised that you are not yet married, Miss Ramsay.'

'Well, I'm not,' she snapped. 'I've not met anyone I've wanted to marry.' She added pettishly, 'I have had several proposals.'

'That does not surprise me.' He smiled down at her, thinking how unusual it was to see grey eyes allied with such very red hair. He sounded suddenly brisk. 'You will do your best to persuade the Colonel to agree to surgery, will you?'

When she nodded, he got into his car and drove away. His handshake had been firm and cool and brief.

Claudia went back to the morning room and found her mother and Dr Willis deep in talk. They smiled at her as she went in, and her mother said, 'He's gone? Such a pleasant man, and not a bit stiff or pompous. Dr

Willis has been telling me that he's quite an important surgeon—perhaps I shouldn't have given him coffee in the kitchen.' She frowned. 'Do you suppose Uncle will take his advice?'

'Most unlikely, Mother. I'll take his lunch up presently, and see if he'll talk about it.'

Great-Uncle William had no intention of talking to anyone on the subject. When Claudia made an attempt to broach the matter, she was told to hold her tongue and mind her own business. Advice which she took in good part, for she was used to the old man's irascible temper and had a strong affection for him.

He had been very good to her mother and to her when her father died, giving them a home, educating her, while at the same time making no bones about the fact that he would have been happier living in the house by himself, with his housekeeper and Tombs to look after him. All the same, she suspected that he had some affection for them both, and was grateful for that.

It was a pity that on his death the house would pass to a distant cousin whom she had never met. That Uncle William had made provision for her mother and herself was another reason for gratitude, for Mrs Ramsay had only a small income, and after years of living in comfort it would have been hard for her to move to some small house and count every penny.

They would miss the old house, with its large rooms and elegant shabbiness, and they would miss Tombs and Mrs Pratt and Jennie too, but Claudia supposed that she would have a job somewhere or other and make a life for herself. Somewhere she could get home easily from time to time. Her mother would miss her friends. Especially she would miss Dr Willis, always there to cope with any small crisis.

The days went unhurriedly by. Claudia finished turn-ing out the library and turned her attention to the rather battered greenhouse at the bottom of the large garden. The mornings were frosty, and old Stokes, who came up from the village to see to the garden, tidied the beds and dug the ground in the kitchen garden, leaving her free to look after the contents of the glass house.

It contained a medley of pots and containers, filled with seedlings and cuttings, and she spent happy hours grubbing around, hopefully sowing seed trays and nurs-ing along the hyacinths and tulips she intended for Christmas.

And every day she spent an hour or so with her great-uncle, reading him dry-as-dust articles from *The Times* or listening to him reminiscing about his military career. He still refused to speak of his illness. It seemed to her anxious eyes that he was weaker, short of breath, easily tired and with an alarming lack of appetite.

Dr Willis came to see him frequently, and it was at the end of a week in which he could detect no improve-ment in his patient that he told Mrs Ramsay that he had asked Mr Tait-Bullen to come again.

He came on a dreary November morning, misty and damp and cold, and Claudia, busy with her seedlings, an old sack wrapped around her topped by a jacket colour-less with age, knew nothing of his arrival. True, she had been told that he was to come again, but no day had been fixed; he was an exceedingly busy man, she'd been told, and his out of town visits had to be fitted in when-ever possible.

He had spent some time with the Colonel, and even longer with Dr Willis, before talking to Mrs Ramsay, and when that lady observed that she would send Tombs to fetch Claudia to join them, volunteered to fetch her himself.

Studying the sack and the old jacket as he entered the greenhouse, he wondered if he was ever to have the pleasure of seeing Claudia looking like the other young women of his acquaintance—fashionably clad, hair immaculate, expertly made up—and decided that she looked very nice as she was. The thought made him smile.

She had looked round as he opened the door and her smile was welcoming.

'Hello—does Mother know you're here?' And then, 'Great Uncle isn't worse?'

'I've seen the Colonel and talked to your mother and Dr Willis. I've been here for some time. Your mother would like you to join us at the house.'

She put down the tray of seedlings slowly. 'Great Uncle William won't let you operate—I tried to talk him into it but he wouldn't listen…'

He said gently, 'I'm afraid so. And the delay has made an operation questionable.'

'You mean it's too late? But it's only a little more than a week since you saw him.'

'If I could have operated immediately he would have had a fair chance of recovering and leading a normal quiet life.'

'And now he has no chance at all?'

He said gravely, 'We shall continue to do all that we can.'

She nodded. 'Yes, I know that you will. I'll come. Is Mother upset? Does she know?'

'Yes.' He watched while she took off the deplorable jacket and untied the sack and went to wash her hands at the stone sink. The water was icy and her hands were grimy. She saw his look. 'You can't handle seedlings in gloves,' she told him. 'They are too small and delicate.'

'You prefer them to dusting books?' he asked as they started for the house.

'Yes, though books are something I couldn't possibly manage without. I'd rather buy a book than a hat.'

He reflected that it would be a pity to hide that glorious hair under a hat, however becoming, but he didn't say so.

Her mother and Dr Willis were in the morning room again, and Mrs Ramsay said in a relieved voice, 'Oh, there you are, dear. I expect Mr Tait-Bullen has explained...'

'Yes, Mother. Do you want me to go and sit with Great-Uncle?'

'He told us all to go away, so I expect you'd better wait a while. Mr Tait-Bullen is going to see him again presently, but he doesn't want anyone else there.' She turned as Tombs came in with the coffee tray. 'But you'll have coffee first, won't you?'

They drank their coffee while the two men sustained the kind of small talk which needed very little reply, and presently Mr Tait-Bullen went back upstairs.

He was gone for some time and Claudia, getting impatient, got up and prowled round the room. 'I don't suppose he'll come again,' she said at length.

'There is no need for him to do so, but the Colonel has taken quite a fancy to him. Mr Tait-Bullen calls a spade a spade when necessary, but in the nicest possible way. What is more, his patients aren't just patients; they are men and women with feelings and wishes which he respects. Your great-uncle knows that.'

Mr Tait-Bullen, driving along the narrow roads which would take him from the village of Little Planting to the

M3 and thence to London, allowed his thoughts to wander. He and the Colonel had talked about many things, none of which had anything to do with his condition. The Colonel had made it clear that he intended to die in his own bed, and, while conceding that Mr Tait-Bullen was undoubtedly a splendid surgeon and cardiologist, he wished to have no truck with surgery, which he considered, at his time of life, to be quite worthless.

Mr Tait-Bullen had made no effort to change his mind for him. True, he could have prolonged his patient's life and allowed him to live for a period at least in moderate health, but he considered that if he had overridden the Colonel's wishes, the old man would have died of frustration at having his wishes ignored. They had parted good friends, and on the mutual understanding that if and when Mr Tait-Bullen had a few hours of leisure he would pay another visit as a friend.

Something he intended to do, for he wanted to see Claudia again.

He went straight to the hospital when he reached London; he had an afternoon clinic which lasted longer than usual. He had no lunch, merely swallowed a cup of tea between patients. It was with a sigh of relief that he stopped the car outside his front door in a small tree-lined street tucked away behind Harley Street, where he had his consulting rooms.

It was a narrow Regency house in a row of similar houses, three storeys high with bow windows and a beautiful front door with a handsome pediment, reached by three steps bordered by delicate iron railings. He let himself in quietly and was met in the hall by a middle-aged man with a craggy face and a fringe of hair. He looked like a dignified church warden, and ran Mr Tait-

Bullen's house to perfection. He greeted him now with a touch of severity.

'There's that Miss Thompson on the phone, reminding you that she expects to see you this evening. I told her that you were still at the hospital and there was no knowing when you'd be home.' Cork lowered his eyes deferentially. 'I trust I did right, sir.'

Mr Tait-Bullen was looking through the post on the hall table. 'You did exactly right, Cork. I don't know what I would do without you.' He glanced up. 'Did I say I would take her somewhere this evening? It has quite slipped my mind.'

Cork drew a deep breath through pinched nostrils. In anyone less dignified it would have been a sniff. 'You were invited to attend the new play. The opening night, I believe.'

'Did I say I'd go? I can't remember writing it down in my diary.'

'You prevaricated, sir. Said if you were free you'd be glad to accept.'

Mr Tait-Bullen picked up his case and opened his study door. 'I'm not free, Cork, and I'm famished!'

'Dinner will be served in fifteen minutes, sir. The young lady's phone number is on your desk.'

Mr Tait-Bullen sat down at his desk and picked up the receiver. Honor Thompson's rather shrill voice, sounding peevish, answered.

'And about time, too. Why are you never at home? It's so late; I'll go on to the theatre and meet you there. The Pickerings are picking me up in ten minutes.'

Mr Tait-Bullen said smoothly, 'Honor, I'm so sorry, but there is absolutely no chance of me getting away until late this evening. I did tell you that I might not be free; will you make my excuses to the Pickerings?'

They talked for a few minutes, until she said, 'Oh, well, you're not much use as an escort, are you, Thomas?' She gave a little laugh. 'I might as well give you up.'

'There must be any number of men queueing up to take you out. I'm not reliable, Honor.'

'You'll end up a crusty old bachelor, Thomas, unless you take time off to fall in love.'

'I'll have to think about that.'

'Well, let me know when you've made up your mind.' She rang off, and he put the phone down and forgot all about her. He had a teaching round the next morning and he needed to prepare a few notes for that.

He ate the dinner Cork set before him and went back to his study to work. He was going to his bed when he had a sudden memory of Claudia, her fiery hair in a mess, enveloped in that old jacket and a sack. He found himself smiling, thinking of her.

The first few days of November, with their frosty mornings and chilly pale skies, had turned dull and damp, and as they faded towards winter Great-Uncle William faded with them. But although he was physically weaker there was nothing weak about his mental state. He was as peppery as he always had been, defying anyone to show sympathy towards him, demanding that Claudia should read *The Times* to him each morning, never mind that he dozed off every now and then.

His faithful housekeeper's endless efforts to prepare tasty morsels for his meals met with no success at all. And no amount of coaxing would persuade him to allow a nurse to attend to his wants. Between them, Claudia, her mother and Tombs did as much as he would allow them to. Dr Willis, inured to his patient's caustic tongue, came daily, but it was less than a week after Mr Tait-Bullen's visit when Great-Uncle William, glaring at him from his bed, observed in an echo of his former commanding tones, 'I shall die within the next day or so. Tell Tait-Bullen to come and see me.'

'He's a busy man...'

'I know that; I'm not a fool.' The Colonel looked suddenly exhausted. 'He said that he would come.' He turned his head to look at Claudia, standing at the window, lingering after she had brought Dr Willis upstairs.

'You—Claudia, go and telephone him. Now, girl!'

She glanced at Dr Willis, and at his nod went down to the hall and dialled Mr Tait-Bullen's number. Cork's dignified voice regretted that Mr Tait-Bullen was not at home.

'It's urgent. Do you know where I can get him?' She added, so as to make things clear, 'I'm not a friend or anything. My great-uncle is a patient of Mr Tait-Bullen's and he wants to see him. He's very ill.'

'In that case, miss, I will give you the number of his consulting rooms.'

She thanked him and dialled again, and this time Mrs Truelove, Mr Tait-Bullen's receptionist, answered.

'Colonel Ramsay? You are his niece? Mr Tait-Bullen has mentioned him. He's with a patient at the moment. Ring off, my dear; I'll call you the moment he's free.'

Claudia waited, wondering if Mr Tait-Bullen would have time to visit Great-Uncle William or even to phone him. She supposed that he was a very busy man; he could hardly be blamed if he hadn't the time to leave London and his patients to obey the whim of an old man who had refused his services. Then the phone rang, and she picked it up.

'Yes,' said a voice in her ear. 'Tait-Bullen speaking.'

This was no time for polite chit-chat. 'Great-Uncle William wants to see you. He says he's going to die in a day or two. He told me to phone you, so I am, because he asked me to, but you don't have to.'

She wasn't sure if she had made herself clear, but apparently she had. Mr Tait-Bullen disentangled the muddle with a twitching lip and answered her with exactly the right amount of impersonal friendliness.

'It is very possible that your great-uncle is quite right. I'm free this evening; I will be with you at about seven o'clock.'

He heard her relieved sigh.

'Thank you very much. I'm sorry if I've disturbed your work.'

'I'm glad you phoned me.'

She could hear the faint impatience in his voice. 'Goodbye, then.' She rang off smartly, and then wondered if she'd been rather too abrupt.

He arrived punctually, unfussed and unhurried. No one looking at his immaculate person would have guessed that he had been up since six o'clock, had missed his lunch and stopped only for the tea and bun his faithful Mrs Truelove had pressed upon him. Dr Willis was waiting for him, and they spent a few minutes talking together before they went up to the Colonel's room. Dr Willis came down presently. 'They're discussing the merits of pyrenaicum aureum as opposed to tenuifolium pumilum...'

Mrs Ramsay looked puzzled. 'Is that some new symptom? It sounds alarming. Poor Uncle William.'

'Lilies,' said Claudia. 'Two varieties of lily, Mother.'

Dr Willis patted her mother's arm. 'Don't alarm yourself, my dear. Your uncle is enjoying his little chat. It was good of Mr Tait-Bullen to come.'

'But he's not doing anything to help Uncle…'

But that was exactly what he *was* doing, reflected Claudia, although she didn't say so. Instead she asked, 'Do you suppose he will stay for supper? Mrs Pratt can grill a couple more chops.'

But when he joined them presently, he declined Mrs Ramsay's offer of supper, saying that he must return to London.

'I hope we haven't spoilt your evening for you—caused you to cancel a date?'

Claudia noticed that he didn't answer that, merely thanked her mother for her invitation. 'If I might have a word with Dr Willis?'

They left the two men, returning when they heard them in the hall.

Mrs. Ramsay shook hands. 'We're so grateful to you. Uncle did so wish to see you again—although I'm sure you are a very busy man.'

He said gravely, 'The Colonel is going to die very soon now, Mrs Ramsay; he is content, and in no pain, and in Dr Willis's good hands.'

He turned to Claudia. 'I was bidden to tell you to read the editorial in *The Times* before he has his supper.' His hand was firm and cool and comforting. 'He's fond of you, you know.'

He left then, getting into his car and driving back to his house to eat the meal Cork had ready for him and then go to his study and concentrate on the notes of the patients upon whom he would be operating in the morning. Before that, he paused to think about the Colonel. A courageous old man hidden behind that crusty manner. He hoped that he would die quietly in his sleep.

Great-Uncle William died while Claudia was still

reading the editorial. So quietly and peacefully that it wasn't until she had finished it that she realised.

She said softly, 'You had a happy talk about lilies, didn't you, Uncle William? I'm glad he came.'

She bent to kiss the craggy old face and went downstairs to tell her mother.

CHAPTER TWO

THE Colonel had been respected in the village; he had had no use for a social life or mere acquaintances, although he had lifelong friends.

Claudia had very little time to grieve. Her mother saw the callers when they came, arranged things with the undertaker and planned the flowers and the gathering of friends and family after the funeral, but it was left to Claudia to carry out her wishes, answer the telephone and make a tidy pile of the letters which would have to be answered later.

Dr Willis was a tower of strength, of course, but he was more concerned with her mother than anything else, and Mrs Ramsay leaned on him heavily for comfort and support. She needed both when, on the day before the funeral, the cousin who was to inherit the house arrived.

He was a middle-aged man, with austere good looks and cold eyes. He treated them with cool courtesy, expressed a token regret at the death of the Colonel and went away to see the colonel's solicitor. When he returned he requested that Mrs Ramsay and Claudia should join him in the morning room.

He stood with his back to the fire and begged them to sit down. Already master of the house, thought Claudia, and wondered what was coming.

He spoke loudly, as though he thought that they were deaf. 'Everything seems to be in order. The will is not yet read, of course, but I gather that there are no surprises in it. I must return to York after the funeral, but

I intend to return within two or three days. Monica—my wife—will accompany me and we will take up residence then. My house there is already on the market. You will, of course, wish to leave here as soon as possible.'

Claudia heard her mother's quick breath. 'Are you interested as to where we are going?'

'It is hardly my concern.' He eyed Claudia coldly. 'You must have been aware for some time that the house would become my property and have some plans of your own.'

'Well,' said Claudia slowly, 'whatever plans we may have had didn't include being thrown out lock, stock and barrel at a moment's notice.' When he started to speak, she added, 'No, let me finish. Let us know when you and your wife will arrive and we will be gone in good time. What about Tombs and Mrs Pratt and Jennie? I understand that they have been remembered in Uncle William's will.'

'I shall, of course, give them a month's wages.' He considered the matter for a moment. 'It might be convenient if Mrs Pratt remained, and the girl. It will save Monica a good deal of trouble if the servants remain.'

'And Tombs?'

'Oh! He's past an honest day's work. He will have his state pension.'

'Have you any children?'

He looked surprised. 'No. Why do you ask?'

She didn't answer that, merely said in a matter-of-fact voice, 'Well, that's a blessing, isn't it?' Then she added, 'I'm glad you're only a distant cousin.'

He said loftily, 'I cannot understand you...'

'Well, of course you can't. But never mind that. Is that all? We'll see you at dinner presently.'

She saw him go red in the face as she got up and urged her mother out of the room.

In the hall, her mother said, 'Darling, you were awfully rude.'

'Mother, he's going to throw Tombs out, not to mention us. He's the most awful man I've ever met. And I'm sure Mrs Pratt and Jennie won't want to stay. I'm going to see them now.'

She gave her mother a reassuring pat on the shoulder. 'Why don't you go and phone Dr Willis and see what he says?'

Over a mug of powerfully brewed tea, she told Tombs and Mrs Pratt and Jennie what her cousin had said. They listened in growing unrest.

'You'll not catch me staying with the likes of him,' said Mrs Pratt. She looked at Jennie. 'And what about you, Jennie, girl?'

'Me neither.' They both looked at Tombs.

Claudia hadn't repeated all her cousin had said about Tombs, but he had read between the lines.

'I'll never get another place at my age,' he told them. 'But I wouldn't stay for all the tea in China.'

He turned a worried old face towards Claudia. 'Where will you and madam go, Miss Claudia? It's a scandal, turning you out of house and home.'

'We'll think of something, Tombs. We've several days to plan something.'

'And Rob?'

'He'll come with us. I don't know about Stokes...'

'I'll see that he gives in his notice,' said Tombs. 'What a mercy that the Colonel isn't here; he would never have allowed these goings on.'

'No, but you see this cousin of his has every right to do what he likes. If you intend to leave when we do, have you somewhere to go? Mother's on the phone to Dr Willis, who may be able to help. If not then we will all put up at the Duck and Thistle in the village.'

'I could go home,' ventured Jennie. 'Me mum'll give me a bed for a bit.' She sounded doubtful, and Claudia said, 'Well, perhaps Dr Willis will know of someone local who needs help in the house. I think we'd all better start packing our things as soon as the funeral is over.'

She found her mother in the morning room. It was cold there, for the fire hadn't been lighted, and Mrs Ramsay was walking up and down in a flurried way.

'Mother, it's too cold for you here, and you're upset.'

'No, dear, there's nothing wrong—in fact quite the reverse. Only I'm not sure how to talk to you about it.'

Claudia sat her parent down on the sofa and settled beside her.

'You talked to Dr Willis? He had some suggestions? Some advice?'

'Well, yes…'

'Mother, dear, does he want to marry you? I know you're fond of each other…'

'Oh, yes we are, love, but how can I possibly marry him and leave you and the others in the lurch? At least…'

'Yes?' Claudia had taken her mother's hand. 'Do tell. I'm sure it's something helpful. He's such a dear; I'll love having him for a stepfather.'

Mrs Ramsay gave a shaky little laugh. 'Oh, darling, will you really? But I haven't said I'd marry him.'

'But you will. Now, what else does he suggest?'

'Well, it's coincidental, but his housekeeper has given him notice—wants to go back to her family somewhere in Lancashire—so Mrs Pratt could take over if she would

like the job. And he knows everyone here, doesn't he?
He says it should be easy to find a place for Jennie.'

'And Tombs?'

'George said he's always wanted a butler. His house
is quite small, but there would be plenty for Tombs to
do. And he'd love to have Rob… Only there's you, darling.'

'But, Mother dear, I'll be getting a job. I've already
applied for several, you know, and none of them are too
far from here. I can come for holidays and weekends, if
George will have me.'

'You're not just saying that to make it easy for the
rest of us?'

'Of course not. You know that was the plan, wasn't
it? That I should come here for a week or two while I
looked for something nearer than London?'

She didn't mention that she had had two answers that
morning from her applications, and both posts had been
filled. There was still another one to come…

'Well, Claudia, if you think that's the right thing to
do. We shall go and tell Tombs and the others.'

'Yes, but no one had better say a word to Mr Ramsay.
When do you see Dr Willis—no, I shall call him George
if he doesn't mind?'

'After the funeral. He thought it best not to come
here.'

'Quite right too. We don't want Cousin Ramsay
smelling a rat. Mother, you go to the kitchen; I'll hang
around the house in case he comes looking for us.'

Later at dinner, Mr Ramsay made no mention of their
plans; he had a good deal to say about the various alterations he intended making in the house. Monica, he
told them, was a woman of excellent taste. She would
have the shabby upholstery covered and the thick velvet

curtains in the drawing room and dining room torn down and replaced by something more up-to-date.

'The curtains were chosen by Great-Uncle William's mother,' observed Mrs Ramsay, 'when she came here as a bride.'

'Then it's high time that they were removed. They are probably full of dust and germs.'

'Most unlikely,' said Claudia quickly. 'Everything in the house has been beautifully cared for.'

He gave her an annoyed look. He didn't like this girl, with the fiery hair and the too ready tongue. He decided not to answer her, but instead addressed Mrs Ramsay with some query about the following day.

It was after the last of the Colonel's friends and ac-quaintances had taken their leave, after returning to the house for tea and Mrs Pratt's delicious sandwiches and cakes, that Mr Potter, the Colonel's solicitor, led the way across the hall to the morning room. He had been a friend of the family for years, and his feelings had been hurt when Mr Ramsay had told him that he would no longer require his services.

His father and his father before him had looked after the Ramsays' modest estate, but he was old himself and he supposed that Mr Ramsay's own lawyer would be perfectly capable. He said now, 'If someone would ask Tombs and Mrs Pratt and Jennie to come in here.' He beamed across at Dr Willis. 'I had already asked you to be present, George.'

He took no notice of Mr Ramsay's frown, but waited patiently until everyone was there.

The will was simple and short. The house and estate were to go to Cousin Ramsay, and afterwards to his heirs. Mrs Ramsay was to receive shares in a company, sufficient to maintain her lifestyle, and Claudia was to receive the same amount, but neither of them could use the capital. Tombs received five thousand pounds, Mrs Pratt the same amount, and Jennie one thousand pounds. Claudia heard Cousin Ramsay draw in a disapproving breath at that.

Mr Potter put the will back in his briefcase and said, suddenly grave, 'If I might have a word with you, Mrs Ramsay, and Claudia, and you, Mr Ramsay?'

When the others had gone, he said, 'I am afraid that I have bad news for you; the company in which the shares were invested and destined for you Mrs Ramsay, and you, Claudia, has gone bankrupt. I ascertained this the day before the Colonel died, and I intended to visit him on that very day. There is nothing to be done about the terms of the will, but perhaps you, Mr Ramsay, will wish to make some adjustment so that Mrs Ramsay and Claudia are not left penniless.'

He saw no sign of encouragement in Mr Ramsay's stern features. Nevertheless he persisted. 'Their incomes would have been small, but adequate. I can advise you as to the amount they would have been. One wouldn't expect you to make good the full amount, but I'm sure that a small allowance for each of them...' His voice faded away under Mr Ramsay's icy stare.

Claudia saw the painful colour in her mother's face. 'That is very thoughtful of you, Mr Potter, but I think that neither mother nor I would wish to accept anything from Mr Ramsay.'

Mr Ramsay looked above their heads and cleared his throat. 'I have many commitments,' he observed. 'Any such arrangement would be quite beyond my means.'

Mr Potter opened his mouth to protest, but Claudia

caught his eye and shook her head. And, although the old man looked bewildered, he closed it again.

It was Mrs Ramsay, who said, in a voice which gave away none of her feelings, 'You'll stay for supper, Mr Potter? I remember Uncle William promised you that little painting on the stairs, which you always admired. Will you fetch it, Claudia?'

She smiled at Mr. Ramsay. 'It is of no value, and one must keep one's promises, must one not?'

Mr Potter refused supper and, clutching the picture, was escorted to his car by Claudia. 'It is all most unsatisfactory,' he told her. 'Your great-uncle would never have allowed it to happen. How will you manage? Surely even a small allowance—'

Claudia popped him into the car and kissed his cheek. 'I'll tell you a secret. Mother is going to marry Dr Willis and I've my eye on a good job. We haven't told Mr Ramsay and we don't intend to. And Tombs and Mrs Pratt and Jennie are all fixed up. So don't worry about us.'

He cheered up then. 'In that case I feel very relieved. You will keep in touch?'

'Of course.'

She waved and smiled as he drove off, then went back into the house. Despite her cheerful words she would hate leaving the old house, although she told herself sensibly that she would have hated staying on there with Mr Ramsay and his wife, who would doubtless alter the whole place so much that she would never recognise it again.

Later, in her mother's bedroom she said, 'You'll have to marry George now, because I told Mr Potter you were going to.'

'But, Claudia, there's nothing arranged...'

'Then arrange it, Mother dear, as quickly as you can. There's something called a special licence, and the vicar's an old friend. Now, what's to happen when we leave? Is George giving us beds, or shall we go to the Duck and Thistle?'

'George wants me to go and see him tomorrow morning. I think he has something planned. Will you stay here, in case Mr Ramsay wants to talk to us about something?'

'Not likely. But I'll be here. Take Rob with you, Mother; *he* doesn't like dogs.'

Mr Ramsay spent the next morning going from room to room, taking careful note of his new possessions. The kitchen and its occupants he ignored; they could be dealt with when he was satisfied with his arrangements. He kept Claudia busy answering his questions about the furniture and pictures, all of which he valued.

'We shall sell a good deal,' he told her loftily. 'There are several pieces which I think may be of real value. But these...' He waved an arm at a pair of Regency terrestrial and celestial globes in one corner of the morning room. 'I doubt if they'd fetch more than a few pounds in a junk shop.'

Claudia, who happened to know that they were worth in the region of twenty thousand pounds and had been in the family for well over a hundred years, agreed politely.

'And this clock—Monica has no liking for such old-fashioned stuff; that can go.' He pointed to a William the Fourth bracket clock, very plain and worth at least two thousand pounds.

He brushed aside a stool. 'And there are all these around. I have never seen such a collection of out-of-date furniture.'

The stool was early Victorian, covered with petit-point tapestry. Claudia didn't mention its value, instead she said politely, 'There is a very good firm at Ringwood, I believe—a branch of one of the London antiques dealers. But I expect that you would prefer to go to someone you know in York.'

'Certainly not. I am more likely to get good prices from a firm which has some knowledge of this area.'

Claudia cast down her eyes and murmured. If and when he sold Great-Uncle William's family treasures, and she could find out who had bought them, she might be able to buy one or two of them back. She had no idea how she would do this, but that was something she would worry about later.

She knew the elder son of the antiques dealer at Ringwood; he might let her buy things back with instalments. Which reminded her of the letter she had stuffed in her pocket that morning. The post mark was Southampton, and it was the last reply from the batch of applications she had sent. Perhaps she would be lucky...

She was roused from her thoughts by Mr Ramsay's sharp, 'Where is your mother?'

She looked at him for a moment before replying. She wondered if she dared to tell him to mind his own business, but decided against it.

'Well, she will have gone upstairs to check the linen cupboard with Mrs Pratt—a long job—then she told me that she would be taking Rob for his walk and doing some necessary shopping in the village. She should be back by lunchtime. I don't know what she will be doing this afternoon.'

He gave her a suspicious glance. 'I wish to inform her of my final plans for moving here.'

'Well, I am going to the kitchen now to see about lunch.'

But first she went into the hall and out of the side door at its end, taking an old coat off a hook as she went and making for the glass house.

The letter was a reply to her application for the post of general helper at a geriatric hospital on the outskirts of Southampton. She had applied for it for the simple reason that there had been nothing else advertised, and she hadn't expected a reply.

Providing that her references were satisfactory, the job was hers. Her duties were vague, and the money was less than she had hoped for, but on the other hand she could start as soon as her references had been checked. It would solve the problem of her immediate future, set her mother's mind at rest and put a little money into her pocket.

She didn't see her mother until the three of them were sitting down to lunch, but she deduced from the faintly smug look on that lady's face that her talk with Dr Willis had been entirely satisfactory. It wasn't until they left the house together to take Rob for another walk that they were able to talk.

'When's the wedding?' asked Claudia as soon as they had left the house.

Her mother laughed. 'Darling, I'm not sure. I won't marry George until you're settled...'

'Then he'd better get a licence as soon as he can. I've got a job—in Southampton at one of the hospitals. I had the letter this morning.'

Mrs Ramsay beamed at her. 'Oh, Claudia, really? I mean, it's something you want to do, not just any old job you're taking to make things easy for us?'

To tell a lie was sometimes necessary, reflected

Claudia, if it was to a good purpose, and surely this was. 'It's exactly what I'm looking for—quite good money and I can come back here for weekends and holidays, if George will have me?'

'Of course we'll have you.' Her mother squeezed her arm. 'Isn't it strange how everything is coming right despite Uncle William's horrid cousin? And George has found a place for Jennie—they were looking for someone up at the Manor, so she will still keep her friends in the village and see Mrs Pratt and Tombs if she wants to.'

'Good. Now, when will you marry?'

'Well, as soon as George can get a licence.'

'You'll stay with him, of course?'

'Mrs Pratt and Tombs will be with me.'

'Mr Ramsay wants to talk to you about his plans. He didn't say anything at lunch...'

'Perhaps this evening.'

He was waiting for them when they got back. 'Be good enough to come to my study?' he asked Mrs Ramsay. 'I dare say Claudia has things to do.'

Dismissed, she went to her room; there were clothes to pack and small, treasured ornaments she had been given since childhood to be wrapped and stowed in boxes. As soon as Mr Ramsay went back to York Dr Willis would come and load up his car and stow everything they didn't want in his attics.

She hoped that the new owner of the house would stay away for several days, for they all intended to be gone, the house empty of people, by the time he and his wife arrived. He had said nothing to Tombs or Mrs Pratt, nor to Jennie; perhaps he expected them to stay on until he saw fit to discharge Tombs. He was arrogant enough to suppose that Mrs Pratt and Jennie would be only too thankful to remain in his service.

Since it was teatime, she went downstairs and found her mother in the morning room. There was no sign of Mr Ramsay, and at her questioning look Mrs Ramsay said, 'He's gone to see the vicar. He's going to York tomorrow afternoon and returning with Monica in two days' time. I am to tell Mrs Pratt and Jennie that they are to stay on in his employment—he hasn't bothered to ask them if they want to—and I'm to dismiss Tombs.'

'Why doesn't he do his own dirty work?' demanded Claudia. 'What else?'

'He avoided asking me where you and I were going; he made some remark about us having friends and he was sure we had sufficient funds to tide us over until we had settled somewhere.'

'Mother, he's despicable. Does he know about you and George?'

'No, I'm sure he doesn't, for he made a great thing of offering to send on our belongings once we had left.'

'Have you had a chance to tell Tombs?'

'No, I'd better go now; if he comes back, come and let me know.'

Not a word was said about their departure during dinner, and the following day Mr Ramsay got into his car and drove himself back to York.

'You may, of course, remain until the day following our return,' he told Mrs Ramsay. 'Monica will wish to be shown round the house.' He looked over her head, avoiding her eyes. 'Kindly see that Tombs has gone by the time we return.'

He turned back at the door. 'It will probably be late afternoon by the time we get here. Tell Mrs Pratt to have a meal ready and see that the maid has the rooms warm.'

Mrs Ramsay lowered her eyes and said, 'Yes,' meekly. She looked very like her daughter. 'I'm sure that if you think of anything else you will phone as soon as you get home.'

They waited a prudent hour before starting on their packing up. He was, observed Claudia, the kind of man who would sneak back to make sure that they weren't making off with the spoons. They collected their belongings, taking only what was theirs, and presently, when Dr Willis drove up, loaded his car. Mr Ramsay had said two days before he returned, but to be on the safe side they had decided to move out on the following day.

Dr Willis would have taken them all to his house for supper, but they refused and, while Mrs Pratt got a meal for them, began on the business of leaving the house in perfect condition. Tombs was set to polish the silver, Jennie saw to the bedrooms, and Claudia and her mother hoovered and dusted downstairs. After supper, tired but happy, they all went to bed.

They were up early in the morning, making sure that there was nothing with which the new owner could find fault, and as soon as the morning surgery was over Dr Willis came to fetch them to his house. He had to make two journeys, and Claudia left last of all, wheeling her bike and leading Rob on his lead. Mr Ramsay had a key—he had taken care to have all of the keys in his possession—but she had a key to the garden door which she had kept. She wasn't sure why and she didn't intend to tell anyone.

Dr Willis's housekeeper had already left, and Mrs Pratt slipped into the kitchen as though she had been there all her life, taking Tombs and Jennie with her.

'There are an awful lot of us,' worried Mrs Ramsay

as they ate the lunch the unflappable Mrs Pratt had produced.

'The house is large enough, my dear, and Jennie goes to her new job tomorrow.'

'And I go to mine in a day or two,' said Claudia.

'You're quite happy about it?' he asked her kindly. 'There's no hurry, you know.'

'It sounds just what I'm looking for. When will you marry? I'd like to come to the wedding.'

'Darling, we wouldn't dream of getting married unless you were there.'

'Within the week, I hope,' said George. 'Very quiet, of course, just us and a few friends here at the church. I've put a notice in the *Telegraph*.'

Everyone in the village knew by now that there was a new owner at Colonel Ramsay's house. Those that had met him didn't like him overmuch. The postman, who had been spoken to sharply by Mr Ramsay because he whistled too loudly as he delivered the letters and had been discovered drinking tea in the kitchen, had promised that any letters would be delivered to the doctor's house. The village considered Mr Ramsay an outsider, for he had made no effort to be pleasant. Even the vicar, a mild and godly man, pursed his lips when his name was mentioned.

There was a letter for Claudia the next morning. Her references had been accepted for the post of general assistant and she should present herself without delay to take up her duties. The list enclosed was vague about these, but the off duty seemed fair enough. She was to have two days a week free and the money was adequate. There was accommodation for her within the hospital.

She wrote back at once, accepting the post, and saying that she would present herself for duty in the early evening of the following day. Feeling pleased that things were turning out so well, she went away to unpack and repack what she would need to take with her.

Dr Willis drove her to Southampton after lunch the following day, and that same afternoon, as dusk was gathering, Mr Ramsay came back to take possession of his new home. An arrogant man, and insensitive to other people's feelings, he had taken it for granted that he would be received suitably—the house lighted and warm, a meal waiting to be put on the table, Mrs Ramsay there to show his wife round, Jennie to see to the luggage. He got out of the car and surveyed the dark, silent house with a frown before unlocking the door.

It was obvious that there was no one there. Monica pushed past him, switched on the lights and looked around her. She saw the letter on the side table and opened it. Mrs Ramsay wrote politely that as Mr Ramsay had requested they had left the house. And, since neither Mrs Pratt or Jennie wished to work for him, they had also left. There was food in the fridge, the fires were laid ready to light and the beds were aired and made up.

Monica laughed. 'You told them you wanted them out, and they've gone. I wonder where they went?'

'It's of no consequence. We can get help from the village easily enough, and I had nothing in common with either Mrs Ramsay or that daughter of hers.'

'A pity about the servants...'

'Easily come by in a small place like this—they'll be only too glad to have the work.'

'There was a butler, you said.'

'Oh, he was too old to work. I dare say he has found himself a room or gone to live with someone. He'd have his pension.'

His wife gave him a long look. 'You're a heartless

man, aren't you? You'd better bring in the luggage while
I find the kitchen and see what there is to eat.'

Dr Willis left Claudia at the door of the hospital with
some reluctance. The place looked gloomy and down at
heel, and he was sorry that he hadn't found out about it
before. True, geriatric hospitals were usually the last
ones to get face lifts—probably inside it was bright and
cheerful enough, and she had wished him goodbye very
happily, with the promise that she would be at the wedding. She poked her head through the open window of
the car.

'I know that you and Mother will be happy. You really are a very nice man, George.'

She picked up her case and went into the hospital.

She knew she wasn't going to like it before she had
gone ten yards from the door, but she ignored that. A
tired-looking porter asked her what she wanted, told her
to leave her case and follow him and led her down a
long passage. He knocked on the door at the end of it.
The label on the door said 'Hospital Manager,' and when
the porter opened the door in answer to the voice inside,
she went past him into a small austere room.

It was furnished sparsely, with a desk and chair, two
other chairs along one wall, and a great many shelves
stuffed with paper files. The woman behind the desk had
a narrow, pale face, a straight haircut in an unbecoming
bob and small dark eyes. She looked up as Claudia went
in, pursing her mouth and frowning a little.

'Miss Ramsay? It's too late for you to do much for
the rest of the day. I'll get someone to show you your
room and take you to where you will be working. But
if you will draw up a chair I will explain your schedule
to you.'

Not a very good start, reflected Claudia, but perhaps the poor soul was tired.

Her duties were many and varied and rather vague. She would work from seven o'clock until three in the afternoon three days a week, and her free day would follow that duty, and for the other three days the hours would be three o'clock in the afternoon until ten o'clock at night.

'The off duty is arranged so that you are free from three o'clock before your day off, and not on duty until three o'clock on the day following.'

Two nights at home, thought Claudia, and felt cheered by the thought.

She asked politely, 'Am I to call you Matron?'

'Miss Norton,' she was told, in a manner which implied that she should have known that without being told. She was dismissed into the care of a small woman with a kind face and a bright smile, who told her that her name was Nurse Symes.

'You're on duty in the morning,' she told her. 'Ward B—that's on the other wing. First floor, thirty beds. Sister Clark is in charge there.'

She paused, and Claudia said encouragingly, 'And…?'

'She's terribly overworked, you know—we can't get the staff. She doesn't mean half she says.'

'Tell me, what exactly do I do? General assistant covers a lot of ground, and Miss Norton was a bit vague.'

'Well, dear, there aren't many trained nurses, so you do anything that's needed.'

They got into the lift at the back of the hall and stepped out on the top floor, went through a door with

'Private' on it and started down another corridor lined with doors.

'Here we are,' said Nurse Symes. 'Quite a nice room, and the bathrooms are at the end. There's a little kitchen too, if you want to make tea.'

The room was small, with a bed, a small easy chair, a bedside table and a clothes cupboard. It was very clean and there was a view of chimneypots from its window. There was a washbasin on one corner, and a small mirror over the wide shelf which served as a dressing table. A few cushions and photos and a vase of flowers, thought Claudia with resolute cheerfulness, and it would be quite pretty.

'We'll go to the linen room and get you some dresses. You'll get three, but of course you'll wear a plastic apron when you're on duty.'

The dresses—a useful mud-brown—duly chosen and taken to her room, they began a tour of the hospital. It was surprisingly large, with old-fashioned wards with beds on either side and tables with pot plants down the centre. The wards were full, and most of the patients were sitting in chairs by their beds, watching television if they were near enough to the two sets at either end of the wards.

Most of them appeared to be asleep; one or two had visitors. Claudia could see only one or two nurses, but there were several young women shrouded in plastic pinnys, carrying trays, mops and buckets and helping those patients who chose to trundle around with their walking aids.

It wasn't quite what she had expected, but it was too early to have an opinion, and first impressions weren't always the right ones.

* * *

It was Cork who folded the *Telegraph* at the appropriate page and silently pointed out the notice of the forthcoming marriage between George Willis and Doreen Ramsay to Professor Tait-Bullen as he ate his breakfast.

He read it in an absent-minded fashion, and then read it again.

'Interesting,' he observed, and then, 'I wonder what will happen to the daughter? Staying on at the Colonel's house, I suppose.'

He thought no more about it until that evening when, urged by some niggling doubt at the back of his mind, he phoned Dr Willis. His congratulations were sincere. 'You will be marrying shortly?'

'In four days' time. Mrs Ramsay is here with me, so are Mrs Pratt and Tombs. Jennie, their maid, went to the Manor to a new job this morning.' George added drily, 'They were turned out by the new owner.'

The professor asked sharply, 'And the daughter— Claudia?'

'Fortunately she found a job at Southampton, in a hospital there—geriatrics. Didn't like the look of the place, but they wanted someone at once.'

'You mean to tell me that this man turned them all out? Is he no relation?'

'A cousin of sorts.'

'Extraordinary.' The professor had a fleeting memory of a lovely girl with red hair and decided that he wanted to know more. 'I'm going to Bristol in a couple of days. May I call in and wish you both well?'

'We'd be delighted. And if you can come to the wedding we should very much like that.'

Mr Tait-Bullen put down the receiver and sat back in his chair. With a little careful planning there was no reason why he shouldn't go to the wedding.

CHAPTER THREE

BY THE end of her first day at the hospital Claudia knew exactly what a general assistant was: a maker of beds, carrier of trays, bedpans, and bags of bed linen. And when she wasn't doing this she was getting the old and infirm in and out of bed, finding slippers, spectacles, dentures, feeding those who were no longer able to help themselves and trotting the more spry of the ladies to the loo.

It was non-stop work, and, going off duty soon after three o'clock, she was thankful that she was free until seven o'clock the next morning and that by some miracle she would have her day off on the day following that. The whole day, she thoughtful joyfully, and not on duty until the afternoon after that. She got into her outdoor clothes and hurried out to the nearest phone box.

Her mother and George were to be married in three days' time; she would be able to go to the wedding, although she would have to leave Little Planting directly after the ceremony. The bus service between Romsey and Southampton was frequent; it was just a question of getting from Romsey to Little Planting and back again.

She would be met, declared her mother; any of their friends in the village would be glad to collect her. 'Phone me tomorrow and let me know what time the bus gets to Romsey. And don't worry about getting back to Southampton, there'll be someone to give you a lift. You're happy there, Claudia?'

'Yes,' said Claudia, 'I'm sure I shall be happy.' She

was so convincing that her mother observed happily to George that Claudia sounded perfectly content, and wasn't it lucky that she should be free for the wedding?

Claudia went back to the hospital and had a cup of tea with some of the other girls, then went to her room, kicked off her shoes and curled up on the bed. Her feet ached and she was tired. It had been a hard day's work, but it wasn't only that; she felt sad and lonely and uncertain of the future. She was prepared to stay in this job for as long as it took to save enough money for her to train in something which would allow her more freedom. Enough money for her to have nice clothes, and a holiday. A career girl.

It would have to be something to do with computers, shorthand and typing and a knowledge of the business world. A receptionist, mused Claudia, a nine-to-five job with free weekends so that she could go and stay with her mother and George from time to time. And, of course, a nicely furnished flat, and friends to entertain and to be entertained by. She might even meet a man who would fall in love with her and marry her...

Mr Tait-Bullen's handsome features imposed themselves upon her wishful thinking, but she brushed them away. One didn't cry for the moon, and she was never likely to meet him again. Even if she did, she wasn't sure if he had noticed her as a woman. She wondered what he was really like behind that impersonal, impassive face. Probably quite nice...

A thump on the door brought her back to reality, and when she called, 'Come in,' a girl opened the door. One of those on the afternoon shift.

'Oh, good, you're here. The other two are out and Sister sent me. Mrs Legge—that's the one with the Zimmer walker—fell over and she's broken a leg and an arm. She'll have to go to the City General with a nurse, and that only leaves Sister and me and we're up to our eyes. Could you come back on duty for an hour or two, just until someone can be found to take over?'

Claudia crammed her feet back into her shoes. It would be, after all, a way of passing the empty evening.

She stayed on the ward for more than two hours, and was sent off at last with the promise of extra time off when it was convenient. She ate supper with several of the other girls, watched television for half an hour and then went to bed. She was too tired to think much. Someone had to look after those old ladies...she would be an old lady herself one day, but hopefully loved and cherished by a husband. Someone like Mr Tait-Bullen, she decided, half asleep.

By the end of the following day she had realised that—never mind what Miss Norton had told her—the off duty was very much in the hands of the ward sister. It was possible, one of the other assistants told her, to have five days in a row of seven o'clock duty, or several days of afternoon shift with no more than an hour or two's notice.

So she wasn't altogether surprised when she was told that she would have an afternoon shift before her day off. That meant she wouldn't be able to go home until the following morning. Still, that would give her all the day before the wedding, and she had already told her mother that she would have to leave directly after the ceremony. She caught the first bus in the morning, after phoning her mother, and found Tombs waiting for her at Romsey. He was driving the doctor's car—a battered old Ford, long ago pensioned off in one corner of the garage, but used in emergencies. It wasn't a long drive, and Tombs filled it with gossip about Mrs

Ramsay, the wedding and how well they had settled in at the doctor's house. Indeed, he seemed to have shed several years; Claudia hadn't seen him as happy for some time, and she was glad of that; she had known him all her life and he was part of it. They talked about the wedding at some length, and he said, 'It is a great pity that you have to return so soon, Miss Claudia. Mrs Ramsay tells me that you have a very good job.'

She enlarged upon that, drawing upon her imagination rather more than was truthful, and was rewarded by his satisfied, 'We all want you to be happy, Miss Claudia.'

At the doctor's house she was greeted by her mother and borne away to inspect the wedding hat, give her opinion of the outfit to go with it and listen while her parent told her of the plans for the wedding.

'Very quiet, of course, but that's how we want it. George can't get away for a week or two, but then we're going down to Cornwall. He has a cottage at St Anthony—that's a bit further on from Falmouth. But we'll be back for Christmas, of course. Will you be able to come home?'

'I don't know, Mother. The off duty is made out a week or two at a time, and it has to be altered from time to time. I'll certainly do my best.'

Christmas was still five weeks or more away; anything could happen...

The wedding was to be at eleven o'clock in the morning. A fellow doctor had come over from a neighbouring village to keep an eye on the practice until the evening, and Mrs Pratt had arranged luncheon for the few friends who had been invited. Tombs, to his tremendous delight, was to give the bride away, and Miss Tremble, who had played the organ for more years than anyone could remember, had insisted on playing for the service.

Claudia, in the grey suit she had had for rather longer than she would have wished, perched a velvet beret on her bright hair and took herself off to the church, leaving her mother and Tombs to follow in George's car.

The handful of friends who had been invited were completely swallowed up by the villagers, who had turned out to a man and woman to see the doctor they respected and liked marry Mrs Ramsay. Claudia, sitting in the front pew greeting those she knew, turned round, craning her neck to see who was there. Almost everyone, except of course Mr and Mrs Ramsay, but they wouldn't have been welcome anyway. She turned round again and looked at George's upright elderly back, and then turned her head once more, this time with everyone else, to watch her mother coming down the aisle, her hand on Tombs' arm.

It was a short, simple service, but what it lacked in grandeur it made up for in warmth and friendliness as the congregation surged down the aisle after the happy pair. Claudia, hemmed in by well-wishers and friends she hadn't seen for some time, looked around her as she waited patiently to leave the church.

At the back of the church Mr Tait-Bullen, towering over those around him, was looking at her. He wasn't smiling, but that didn't prevent her from feeling pleasure at the sight of him. She made her way towards him and held out a hand.

'Hello, how nice to see you here. Did George invite you?'

He took her hand, shook it briskly and gave it back to her. 'I invited myself. I saw the notice in the *Telegraph* and, since I am on my way to Bristol, George kindly suggested that I might like to come to the church.'

They were outside now, everyone getting into cars or walking back to the doctor's house.

'You're coming to the house?'

'Yes.' Without asking her, he opened the car door and popped her in. 'Are you still at the Colonel's house? George said something about you leaving…'

He didn't sound very interested, so all she said was, 'Yes, we have all left.'

'And you?'

'Oh, I've got a job at Southampton. I'm going back this afternoon.'

They had reached the doctor's house, and Mr Tait-Bullen parked the car, opened her door and followed her inside. They were separated almost at once by other guests, and, feeling let down that he had evinced so little interest in her, Claudia wormed her way to where her mother and George were standing.

She kissed them both. 'I know you're going to be happy,' she told them. 'And this is a lovely wedding; everyone here wants you to be happy too.'

Her mother beamed at her. 'Darling, it's such a wonderful day. Must you go back so soon?'

'I'm afraid so. I'm on duty at three o'clock. I must get to Romsey in time to catch the bus, it goes at a quarter past the hour. Could Tombs take me?'

'Of course he can. And if he can't there are plenty of people here who wouldn't mind running you over to Romsey.' Her mother frowned. 'I meant to have fixed something up, but there was so much to do and think about…'

'Don't worry, Mother. And it will be a pity to take Tombs away; he's being so useful here. I'll get Tom Hicks from the garage to run me over.'

It was ten minutes or so later when she went back to

the buffet with the plate of canapés she had been hand-
ing round, that she found Mr Tait-Bullen beside her. He
took the plate from her, put it back on the table and
handed her a glass of champagne. He said pleasantly,
'I'll drive you to Southampton. When do you want to
leave?'

'But you're not going to Southampton; you're going
to Bristol. You said so.'

'Indeed I am, but I have ample time to take you back
on my way. At what time do you need to leave here?'

'I'm on duty at three o'clock. I was going to catch a
bus from Romsey. There's really no need—it's very kind
of you, but you'll miss the rest of the reception.'

Looking at him, she could see that he was taking no
notice of what she was saying. He said now, 'If we leave
at half past one that should give us ample time.
Presumably you will need time to get ready for whatever
job you are in.'

'I'm a general assistant at a geriatric hospital. It's near
the docks.'

She spoke defiantly, as though she expected him to
argue with her, but all he said was, 'You'll have to guide
me. Do you like your work?'

'Yes. I've only been there for a short while. It's—it's
very interesting.'

The vicar joined them then, and presently she excused
herself and went to talk to Mr Potter, who asked her
worriedly if she was managing.

'I hear you have work at Southampton. Providential,
my dear, providential. I have been worried about you
and your mother, and can only be thankful that things
have turned out so well for you both.'

'Oh, everything is splendid,' said Claudia. 'And Dr
Willis has been so kind and thoughtful to all of us.'

'You have not seen Mr and Mrs Ramsay since they returned to the house?'

'No, and I don't want to.' She patted his arm. 'We don't need to worry about them any more, Mr Potter. We hated leaving the house, but we couldn't have stayed even if he had suggested it.'

She wandered round the room then, talking to other guests, most of them old friends who had known her for years. But she kept her eye on the clock, and when she saw that it had just struck one, she went in search of her mother and George, wished them goodbye, assured them that Mr Tait-Bullen was driving her back, and promised to come again just as soon as she had a free day.

Then she got her case and went into the hall. Tombs was there, talking to Mr Tait-Bullen as he shrugged himself into his coat.

'Ah, there you are, Miss Claudia. I was just saying you'd be here dead on time, and so you are.'

'Tombs, it's been a lovely wedding, and I'm sure you did a great deal to make it so. I'll be back when I get a day off. Take care of yourself, won't you? I've seen Mrs Pratt and Jennie.'

'Bless you, miss,' said Tombs, and opened the door for them. 'A safe journey.'

Claudia settled herself in the comfortable seat. 'Do you know how to get onto the Romsey road? Through the village and keep straight on, then turn left at the crossroads. Then it's a right-hand fork. The roads are narrow.'

He said thank you so meekly that she was emboldened to say chattily, 'We're so glad that George gave Tombs a job. He'd been with my great-uncle for years and years. I don't suppose there are many like him...'

Mr Tait-Bullen, not a man for small talk, gave a grunt.

And, since he had nothing to say, Claudia observed, 'Are you one of those people who don't like to talk while they are driving? I dare say it takes quite a lot of concentration, especially in a car like this one.'

Mr Tait-Bullen, whose work demanded powers of concentration well beyond the average, gave another grunt.

Claudia, not one to give up easily, took a look at his profile. It looked severe. 'Oh, well, if you don't want to talk...' She turned her head to look out of the window. 'Probably you're tired.'

'No, I am not in the least tired. Claudia, tell me your off duty for next week...'

'Whatever for?' When he didn't answer, she said, 'Oh, well...' and told him. 'But it gets changed at the last minute very often. There don't seem to be enough staff...'

'It is not, I believe, the most popular form of nursing.'

'Oh, I can quite see that, and I'm not even a nurse.'

'You say that you will be free at three o'clock on Friday? I shall call for you shortly after that and we will spend the rest of the day together.'

'Oh, will we? Have I been asked?'

'Ah, forgive me. I presumed that you would like to see me again, just as I would like to see you.'

'Well!' exclaimed Claudia. 'Whatever next...?'

'Just so. That is what I wish to find out.'

A remark which needed to be thought about and still remained puzzling.

'Well, thank you,' said Claudia, deciding to ignore his remark for the moment. 'But don't be annoyed if my off duty's been changed.'

'I don't think you need worry about that.'

They were threading their way through the outskirts

of Southampton. 'Tell me where I should turn off?' he said.

It was half past two when he stopped before the hospital entrance. He got out to open her door and walked with her into the entrance hall. He handed her case over, and when she put out a hand shook it briefly.

'Thank you for the lift.' She smiled up at him and he smiled in return, a slow, gentle smile so that he looked quite different from the rather silent reserved man she had thought him to be. And the smile warmed her loneliness, making the future full of unexpected hope. It wasn't until then that she realised how much she needed a friend.

When she had gone, Mr Tait-Bullen strolled over to the old-fashioned porter's lodge. He was there for several minutes, until its elderly occupant led him away down a long, dreary corridor, knocked on a door and ushered him inside.

Claudia didn't exactly forget him for the rest of the day; he was there at the back of her mind, almost smothered in her non-stop chores. The old ladies were such a cruel contrast to the pleasures of the morning she could have wept with pity for them. Not that weeping would have helped in any way: cups of tea, endless trundles to the loo, mopping up after the inevitable accidents, making beds and the back-breaking task of getting elderly frail bodies back into bed... By ten o'clock, when she went off duty, her mother's wedding seemed part of a dream.

She fell into bed and was instantly asleep. In the morning, after a quick shower, she got into the brown dress and went down to her breakfast, her spirits fully restored. And they stayed that way all day, despite the hundred and one setbacks and Sister's sharp tongue.

Claudia forgave her that, for coping with forty old ladies, keeping them clean and tidy and well fed, was no easy task. Claudia, putting clean sheets on a bed for the umpteenth time, considered Sister a splendid woman, even if she had no time to waste on being friendly.

All the same, it was difficult not to feel hard done by when that lady told her that her Friday off duty would be altered; she was to go on the afternoon shift instead of the morning. She wouldn't be able to go out with Mr Tait-Bullen after all, and there was no way of letting him know. She hoped that he wouldn't be too annoyed about it; not to annoy him was suddenly important. Not that it mattered any more. He would go away and not bother to see her again. That thought left her feeling sad.

She was going off duty the next day when Sister called her into the office.

'You'll take your original off duty on Friday.' She sounded cross. 'There will be an extra nurse here for a couple of days, so there will be no need for you to change.'

'I shall be free at three o'clock on Friday?' asked Claudia, just to make sure.

'I've just said so, haven't I? You young girls are all alike, never listening to a word that is said to them.'

Claudia begged her pardon in a suitably humble voice, and once out of the office did a few dance steps along the corridor. Maybe the future wasn't going to be so bad, after all.

Friday dawned wet and cold. Claudia, deep in her morning chores, found the time to look out of the windows in the hope that the weather would improve. It did no such thing. Indeed a nasty wind had sprung up. It would have to be the grey suit and a raincoat—both suitable for the conditions out of doors, but hardly likely to inspire Mr Tait-Bullen to take her anywhere fashionable for tea.

She thought that three o'clock would never come, and even if it did, would she get off duty punctually? She did, hurrying through the hospital to her room, in a panic that she would be called back at the last moment.

Once there, she didn't waste a second—tearing out of the brown uniform, racing to the shower room before someone else got there, dressing with the speed of light. He had said shortly after three o'clock, but if she didn't show up within fifteen minutes of that time she hardly hoped that he would wait much longer. It was already five minutes over time as she gained the entrance hall, out of breath, and with her hair bundled up underneath the velvet beret. There had been no time to do more than powder her nose and put on some lipstick. She didn't look her best, she worried. He would take one look at her and decide that he was wasting his time...

Mr Tait-Bullen, leaning his length against a marble bust of a bewhiskered Victorian dignitary, entertained no such thought. He watched her slither to a dignified walk as she crossed the hall and reflected that she was the most beautiful girl that he had ever set eyes on. Even in the unbecoming garment in which she was swathed. But then she would look mouthwatering in a tablecloth with a hole cut for her head.

None of these interesting thoughts showed on his face as he went to meet her.

'Hello,' said Claudia, her smile so enchanting that he had difficulty in keeping his hands to himself. 'I haven't kept you waiting? I was so afraid that you might think I wasn't coming.' She plucked a bright lock of hair which had escaped her brush and tucked it behind an ear. 'I haven't done my hair properly.' She searched his calm face. 'I'm not dressed up either. You don't mind?'

'No, I don't mind. You look very nice.'

A tepid compliment which satisfied her; he had smiled at her when he had made it, which gave her a comfortable feeling that he had meant exactly what he had said.

'Shall we have tea first? I thought we might drive into the country for dinner later.'

'That would be lovely. Nowhere grand—I'm not dressed for it. I mean, I didn't know if we would be going out this evening—I was in a hurry so's not to miss you...' She paused, aware that she was babbling.

He said gently, 'There's a nice quiet hotel at Wickham. But tea first.'

He drove into the heart of Southampton and took her to a small quiet tea room tucked away in a side-road where he was able to park the car. The place was half-full, warm and pleasantly lighted, and they sat down at a table in the window curtained against the gathering dark of the late afternoon.

They ate hot buttered teacakes, and Claudia, urged to do so, sampled the creamy confections the waitress brought, and all the while Mr Tait-Bullen kept up an undemanding flow of small talk, calculated to put her at her ease so that presently, warm and nicely full, she answered his carefully put questions with less caution than she might have done.

Yes, it was hard work, she admitted, but the other girls were friendly and most of the old ladies were dears. 'Although there are one or two who are a bit difficult...'

'In what way?'

'Oh, they don't mean to be. They get cross, but I'd get cross if I had to sit in a chair because I couldn't do anything for myself. You see, they don't seem to have anyone to look after them—if they had daughters or someone, or sons or husbands who could look after them…'

'That might be difficult in a household with children, or where everyone goes out to work.'

'Yes, I know. Only it would be nice.'

Her hand was lying on the table, and he saw that it was rough and rather red. He said lightly, 'I dare say you have a lot of mopping up to do.'

'Oh, yes. All the time.' She smiled suddenly. 'It's not the cool hand on the brow kind of work—more like a charwoman—plastic pinnys and mops and buckets.'

'You intend to stay there?'

'When I've saved up enough money I shall train for something…' She saw his raised eyebrows. 'Well, I don't know what yet.' She paused. 'I'm talking too much. Will you tell me about you?'

'I live and work in London. I have a house there, and Cork, who has been with me for a long time, looks after me. I have patients in several hospitals and hold clinics in each of them. I have a private practice, and I operate twice a week—sometimes three times. I travel round the country from time to time if I'm wanted for a consultation or to operate.'

'You have lots of friends?'

'I have a few old friends and acquaintances, yes. I'm not married, Claudia.'

She went pink. 'I should have asked you that ages ago, shouldn't I? I did want to, but I—well, I don't know you well enough…'

'We must do something about that. At what time do you have to be back?' And when she told him he said, 'Good, we'll drive to Evershot for dinner. It's a pleasant drive, even in the dark, and we have no need to hurry.'

At her uncertain look, he added, 'Don't worry, it's a quite small hotel. At this time of the year it will be half-empty, and it isn't somewhere where one needs to dress up.'

They went back to the car then, and he drove through the heavy evening traffic until they had left the city behind, taking the secondary roads through the New Forest. Mr Tait-Bullen drove slowly, stopping from time to time to allow the ponies to cross the road ahead of him, and a badger to amble along, refusing to be hurried. He drove for the most part in silence, an easy, undemanding silence in which there was no need to talk for the sake of uttering.

Claudia sat cocooned in warmth and comfort and watched the road unwind ahead of them in the car's headlights. She hadn't felt so quietly happy for a long time.

Evershot was a sizeable village, and even on a dark, wintry night looked charming. The hotel was charming too—not large, but delightfully furnished, warm and welcoming. They went to the bar and sat over drinks, then dined on crab ravioli with ginger, breast of duck with potato straws and tiny brussels sprouts, and pear tatin with cinnamon ice cream. Claudia ate it all with a splendid appetite, sharpened by the wholesome, rather stodgy fare offered at the hospital.

She sat back, savouring the last mouthful of ice cream. 'That was lovely—and do you know it was just luck that I was free this afternoon? Sister changed my duty to the afternoon shift, and then she changed her mind. It was a miracle...'

Mr Tait-Bullen, who had engineered the miracle, agreed that indeed it was.

They sat over their coffee and Claudia, gently encouraged by her companion, talked. There was not much time to talk at the hospital—really talk. On duty conversations were confined to cheerful chat with those of the patients who welcomed it, and only that when there were a few minutes to spare. And off duty, although she got on well with the other girls, the inclination was either to go out or to sit in front of the television. But now she allowed her tongue full rein, vaguely aware that later on she would regret it but happy now, saying whatever came into her head. She paused briefly.

'Am I boring you?'

'No. I do not think that you will ever bore me, Claudia. I have to go away for a couple of days. When I return I should like to take you out again.'

'Oh, would you? I'd like that too.' She beamed at him. 'We get on well together, don't we? I didn't think I would like you when we met, but I've changed my mind.'

'I hoped that you would. As you say, we get on well together.'

He drove her back presently, saw her into the hospital and, under the porter's interested eye, bent to kiss her cheek. It wasn't until she was in her room that she realised that he hadn't said anything more about seeing her again.

Claudia, brushing her fiery locks, stopped to stare into the small mirror above the little dressing table.

'You're a fool,' she told her reflection. 'Whatever he said, he must have been bored out of his mind. I must have sounded like a garrulous old maid. No wonder he didn't say when he would want to see me again.' She put down the brush and got into bed, suddenly sad; she liked him and felt at ease in his company. If only she hadn't behaved like an idiot. Living in London, obviously a successful man in his profession, and presumably comfortably off, she thought gloomily, he would have his pick of elegant women who had a fund of witty and amusing talk and knew when to hold their tongues...

Two days later she was on the afternoon shift. It was drizzling outside, with a mean wind, and the thought of a morning doing nothing by the gas fire in the recreation room was tempting. Then Claudia thought of the long hours on the ward until the late evening, buttoned herself into her mac, tied a scarf over her hair, found her gloves and sensible shoes and made her way to the side door the hospital staff used. A brisk walk would do her good...

She was crossing the back of the hall when the porter called after her.

'I've been ringing round for you,' he grumbled. 'You're to go to the visitors' room.'

'Me? Why?'

'How should I know? That's the message I got and I'm telling it to you.'

'Yes—well, thank you!'

She turned round and went the other way along the wide corridor from which the boardroom, the manager's office and the consultants' room opened.

'Mother,' she said, suddenly afraid of bad news, and opened the door.

The room didn't encourage visitors. It was a dark brown, with shiny lino on the floor and a hideous glass lantern housing a stark white bulb glaring down onto the solid table beneath it. Chairs were arranged stiffly around the walls, and, half lost in the massive fireplace, there was a very small gas fire. Watching her from the other side of the table was Mr Tait-Bullen.

Claudia slithered to a halt. 'Oh, it's you.' And then,

aware that perhaps that had sounded rude, added, 'What I meant is, I didn't expect you.' He smiled then, and she smiled back. 'I was just going out for a walk.'

When he didn't speak, she asked, 'Are you on your way somewhere or are you on holiday?'

'I'm on my way back to London.'

'Well, what luck I'm on afternoon duty.' She flushed. 'What I mean is, you could have called in and I would have been working.' She hurried on, because it sounded as though she expected him to take her out. 'I expect you're anxious to get back home...'

'In which case I should have driven straight back to London...'

'But you didn't know if I was free...'

'Yes, I did. I phoned up first to find out. I have to go away again for a couple of days, and I wanted to see you before I go.'

'Me? Why? Mother's not ill, or George? Did they ask you to come?'

'No, they are both, as far as I know, in the best of middle-aged health.'

He smiled at her, a slow, warm smile. 'Claudia, before I say anything more, will you answer me truthfully? Are you happy here? Are you content to be, eventually, a career girl and, if not, will you tell me what you really wish for?'

'Why do you want to know?' she asked, and, when he didn't answer, went on, 'Well, all right—no, I'm not happy here. I'm truly sorry for the old ladies, but I miss the garden and the village and being out of doors. We're well looked after, you know, but I feel trapped.' She had lost herself in her own thoughts. 'And I suppose I wish for what every woman wants—a home and a husband and children.'

'Not love?'

'That too, but I think that isn't granted to everyone—I mean, the kind of love that doesn't mind being poor or neglected or kept hidden, and will love and cherish despite that.' She stopped suddenly. 'Why did you make me say all that?'

He didn't answer her at once, but stared at her across the table, seeing a rather untidy figure, her bright hair escaping from the scarf, enveloped in her sensible mac.

'Will you marry me, Claudia?' he asked quietly.

At her astonished look, he said, 'No, don't say anything for a moment or two. You see, I think we might have a successful and happy marriage. I need a wife and you long for freedom. We could help each other in many ways; I have no doubt that you will be an excellent housewife and hostess, and a companion I shall always enjoy, and you could be free to spread your wings in whichever direction you wish to fly.

'I haven't said that I love you, nor do I expect you to tell me that. There's time enough for us to get to know each other. And I shan't hurry you. But it seems to me that to marry as soon as possible would be the sensible thing to do. You will need to give a week's notice at the hospital, but there is no reason why we shouldn't marry before Christmas.'

Claudia opened her mouth to speak, and shut it again, reflecting on what he had said. It all sounded so sensible, so calmly thought out. And he didn't love her. On the other hand he must like her, if he intended to marry her, and she would enjoy having a household of her own—meeting people, making friends, being there when he wanted a companion. And she liked him; she liked him very much.

Mr Tait-Bullen asked quietly, 'You would like to

think about it? I shall quite understand if you dislike the idea, but I shall be disappointed. You see, Claudia, I have been honest with you. I have not promised love and endless devotion, but I have offered you what I hope will be a happy and contented life together. We like the same things, don't we? And laugh at the same jokes. We would be good companions and friends. That, I think, is more important than a sudden and uncertain infatuation.'

He was right, of course. It was, she told herself, a sensible and sincere offer of marriage made by one of the handsomest men she had ever met, and a man she liked wholeheartedly. She didn't know much about him, but, as he had said, getting to know each other was something they could do in their own good time. She would be a good wife, just as she was instinctively aware that he would be a good husband.

She looked across the table at him, standing there with no sign of impatience.

'Yes, thank you, I should like to marry you.' She laughed suddenly. 'I don't know your name...'

He came round the table and put gentle hands on her shoulders. 'Thomas,' he said, and bent to kiss her. 'Thank you, Claudia.'

CHAPTER FOUR

CLAUDIA looked up into his quiet face. 'What do we do next?'

Mr Tait-Bullen suppressed a smile. A girl after his own heart; no coy smiles and fluttering of the eyelashes, no girlish whispers. Claudia obviously liked to meet a situation, when she encountered it, head-on.

'If you will give in your notice today? Phone me this evening—I'll be in Edinburgh; I'll give you my number—let me know the soonest you can leave and I'll fetch you.'

'Where will I go?'

'To George Willis. We'll marry there if you would like that. I'll get a special licence—remind me to ask you for some particulars when you phone. Your mother?'

'I'll phone her.'

'A pity that I have to go back to town this morning; I could have called in at Little Planting. I'll telephone her this evening.'

He was holding her hands in his. 'This must be the most unlikely place in the world in which to receive a proposal of marriage.'

'I don't think that matters at all. I mean, moonlight and roses wouldn't have been suitable, would they? Not for us.'

He frowned a little. 'You will be happy, Claudia? I am a good deal older than you...'

'I like you just as you are, Thomas. Please don't change any of you. We shall be happy together.'

'I must go. Forgive me, there isn't even time to give you a cup of coffee.'

She went with him to the hospital entrance and he kissed her again, a light kiss which meant nothing, although she hadn't expected it to, got into his car and drove away.

It was a few moments before she moved—back into the hospital, intent on doing what Thomas had suggested, not noticing the porter's interested stare. She must compose a suitable letter and then take it to Miss Norton, and she must do it at once, so that when Thomas phoned that evening she could tell him when she could leave. And she must phone her mother...

She wrote her letter of resignation and presented herself at Miss Norton's office, inwardly quaking; could she be prevented from leaving? She hadn't signed a contract, and she was paid weekly, all the same she wasn't absolutely sure...

Fifteen minutes later she closed the office door behind her with a sigh of relief. Miss Norton hadn't been very pleased. Indeed, she had read Claudia a lecture on young women who were irresponsible and said she hoped that she had given marriage serious thought, but she hadn't refused to let Claudia go. She was, she had pointed out, scrupulously fair in such matters; if a girl wasn't happy in her work then she was entitled to leave. Normally, said Miss Norton severely, after a reasonable period. Claudia had hardly given herself time to settle down, but in the circumstances she could, of course, leave.

Claudia had thanked her and asked if she could leave two days earlier, since she would have her week's days off due. Miss Norton had looked affronted but she had agreed.

Claudia got into her mac again and went to telephone her mother; there was a phone in the hospital, but it was in a passage and in constant use; to discuss anything other than the weather was impossible.

Her mother was delighted, surprised as well. 'Darling, I didn't know that you and Mr Tait-Bullen—Thomas— were so close. I'm delighted, and I'm sure George will be too when I tell him. What are your plans?'

Claudia inserted all the money she had, and explained. 'And we want to have a very quiet wedding, Mother. Thomas is getting a special licence and we'd like to marry at Little Planting. I'm leaving in five days; Thomas will fetch me. May I stay with you and George until the wedding? It'll only be for a day or two.'

'Of course, darling. And we must do something about clothes...'

Claudia, with an inward eye on her scanty wardrobe, agreed.

The rest of the day passed in a dream; since she was happy, she wanted everyone else to be happy too, coaxing smiles from even the most cantankerous of the old ladies, clearing up unmentionable messes, changing sheets, trundling round the ward with the tea trolley, the supper trolley and at the end of the day having to listen to a lecture from Sister, who, apprised of her leaving, took it as a personal affront.

It was after ten o'clock by the time she left the ward— too late to go to the phone box at the end of the road. Besides, the passage where the hospital phone was was empty so late in the evening. She rang the number Thomas had given her and waited, half afraid that he wouldn't answer.

His voice sounded strangely businesslike.

'It's me,' said Claudia, heedless of grammar. And she added quite unnecessarily, 'You told me to ring you up, but I haven't kept you up, have I?'

Mr Tait-Bullen, studying the notes of a patient he was to operate on the next day, assured her that she hadn't.

'You saw Miss Norton?'

'Yes, I may leave in five days' time—actually, it's four days now. That's a Friday.'

'In the morning? You're actually free to leave after duty on Thursday?'

'Yes, but I must pack my things and give my uniform back…'

'I'll come for you at nine o'clock on Friday morning, Claudia.'

'Thank you, but don't you have to work?'

He said gently, 'Oh, yes, but not until the afternoon, I'll drop you off at Little Planting on my way back. Now, tell me—where were you born, how old are you, have you any other names besides Claudia, and are you British by birth?'

She told him in a matter-of fact voice, sensing that he hadn't time to waste on idle talk. She hesitated before she said, 'My other name is Eliza…' and waited for him to laugh.

But he didn't. All he said was, 'That's a nice old-fashioned name. You must be tired, my dear. Get to bed and sleep well. I'll see you on Friday.'

'Good night, then,' Claudia said, and hung up. It would have been nice if he had said something like, I miss you, or, I'm looking forward to seeing you. But he wouldn't pretend to feelings he didn't feel; she quite understood that. Theirs would be a sensible marriage, she reflected, undressing and falling into bed, there would be no false sentiment.

The following afternoon she took herself off to the shops; she hadn't much money, but it was essential that she had something suitable in which to be married. Luck was on her side; she found a small dress shop going out of business and selling up at half price. Claudia thrust aside a wish to wear white chiffon and a gauzy veil and tried on a plainly cut dress and jacket in finc wool. It was in a misty blue, with a grey velvet collar and cuffs, and fastened with a row of velvet buttons. And when the saleslady found a charming hat in matching velvet, Claudia decided that she need look no further.

'It's for a special occasion?' enquired the sales lady.

'Well, yes—my wedding.'

Which prompted the sales lady, who had a sentimental heart under her smart black dress, to make a special price. And that meant that there was enough money left to buy gloves and shoes—and some essential underpinnings from Marks and Spencer.

Well pleased with her purchases, Claudia went back to thc hospital—too late for tea and too early for supper, but that didn't matter. She tried everything on once more and spent a long time trying out various new hairstyles, none of which pleased her. Perhaps once she was married she would be able to go to a good London hairdresser and have it expertly cut.

The days dragged; Friday was never coming, and she had ample time to wonder if she was about to make the mistake of a lifetime. A letter or a phone call from Thomas would have cleared up her uncertainty, but there was nothing. He had told her that he would see her on Friday and with that she had to be content. She had phoned her mother again, and that lady, agog with maternal delight, had told her that she was to go with her to Salisbury and get a few clothes. 'Our wedding present to you, darling. Have you bought anything yet?'

Claudia described the dress and jacket.

'They sound just right. Aren't you excited? And will you have a honeymoon?'

'No. Thomas can only take a day off—we'll go later.'

On the Thursday she bade the old ladies goodbye, leaving a vase filled with chrysanthemums on one of the tables, wishing she could have done more to brighten the ward. Sister wished her goodbye in an ill-humoured way, and then surprised her by saying, 'A pity you are leaving; the old ladies liked you.'

And the other girls were friendly—laughing and joking and asking her to send photos of the wedding.

'Well, it's not that kind of wedding,' she explained. 'Just us and a few family and no one else...'

'Who'd want anyone else but him, anyway?' declared one of the girls, who had seen Mr Tait-Bullen leaving the hospital. Everyone laughed and Claudia got out a bottle of sherry and a packet of biscuits. It seemed the right moment for a farewell party.

She was ready and waiting long before nine o'clock the next morning. Supposing Thomas had changed his mind? Had a breakdown, an accident, been called away to an emergency? She sat, as still as a mouse, wrapped in the mac, since it was raining again, her hair glowing in the gloomy entrance hall.

Mr Tait-Bullen knew exactly how she felt the moment he set eyes on her.

He nodded to the porter and reached her before she could get to her feet, his eyes searching her face. What he saw there reassured him, and he smiled.

'I can see that I am marrying a treasure. Do you know that the one virtue a medical man longs for in a wife is punctuality? You see, he is never punctual himself...'

'I was a bit early. I wasn't sure—that is, I thought that perhaps...' She met his steady gaze. 'No, that's not quite true—I knew you'd come.'

'Of course. Do you have to see anyone? You've said your goodbyes?'

And, when she nodded, he picked up her case and together they left the hospital.

They were clear of Southampton, driving through a dripping countryside, before he said, 'If you will agree, we can be married on Monday. I'll come down to Little Planting on Sunday evening, and we can marry in the morning and drive back in the afternoon.'

He had a list on Tuesday, but there would be Monday evening in which to show Claudia her new home. Cork had confided plans for a splendid supper, and Mr Tait-Bullen had left his devoted servant icing a cake for tea. It wasn't the kind of wedding that Cork would have liked for his master, but he was determined to make it as bridal an occasion as possible.

And that reminded him of something. He brought the car to a gentle halt and fished around in a pocket.

'Ours must be one of the briefest engagements ever known,' he observed, and opened the little velvet box in his hand. The ring it contained was a sapphire, a rich, sparkling blue surrounded by diamonds and mounted in gold. He picked up Claudia's left hand, resting in her lap, took off her glove and slipped the ring on her finger.

'Oh, it's beautiful—and it fits.' Claudia's sigh was one of pure delight. 'Thank you, Thomas.' She stared at it, incongruous on her roughened hand with its short, clipped nails. She would have to do something about that before the wedding.

She looked at him and saw that he was studying her hand. She said quite awkwardly, 'We did wear gloves whenever we could, but sometimes it just wasn't possible.'

His smile was kind. 'It was my grandmother's engagement ring. She left it to me with the wish that I would give it to the girl I married.'

'She was fond of you?'

'Indeed, she was; we were the best of friends.'

'You miss her?'

'Yes, we all do—my mother and father, my two sisters and younger brother. You will meet them all at Christmas…'

Claudia said faintly, 'Oh, shall I? Do they all live in London?'

'No, Mother and Father live in Cumbria, a small village called Finsthwaite, at the southern end of lake Windermere. It is rather remote but very beautiful, close to the heart of Grizedale Forest but not too far from Kendal. My sisters are married. Ann—she's the elder—lives in York; her husband's a solicitor. Amy and her husband live near Melton Mowbray; he's a farmer. James is at Birmingham Children's hospital—a junior registrar.'

'They won't be coming to our wedding?'

'Mother and Father—the rest of the family you'll meet at Christmas. We shall spend it at Finsthwaite.' He added casually, 'They'll be delighted to welcome you into the family.'

'They don't know me. They might not like me…'

'You will be my wife,' said Thomas.

A fact which she could not dispute.

Tombs, beaming widely, opened the door to them when they reached George's house. He shook Claudia by the hand, and then Mr Tait-Bullen, wished them happy and led them across the hall to the sitting room. Her mother was there and embraced Claudia warmly before offering a cheek for her future son-in-law.

'Such a surprise,' she told them. 'We're all so excited. George is in his surgery but Tombs has gone to fetch him. We had no idea...'

Nor had I, thought Claudia, but she didn't say so. 'We thought we'd be married on Monday...'

'Darling—but you haven't any clothes, and I must have a new hat at least, and who is to be invited? Such short notice...'

'Thomas would like his parents to come, Mother.' Claudia looked at him and felt a touch of peevishness at the sight of him standing there, looking faintly amused.

'May they do that, Mrs Willis? We both want a quiet wedding, and I can't spare more than a day. We would like to marry in the morning, then drive back to London, which would give us the rest of the day together.'

'Of course, you poor dears—scarcely more than a few hours to be together.'

'We shall make up for that later on,' said Mr Tait-Bullen soothingly.

He turned as George came into the room. 'We do hope we haven't spoilt any plans you and Mrs Willis may have made...'

Dr Willis kissed Claudia and shook hands with him. 'We don't go away until the end of next week, and even if we had plans we would be delighted to upset them for such a happy occasion. Staying for lunch, I hope?'

Tombs had brought in the coffee tray, and Mrs Willis

poured while Claudia, glad of something to do, handed around cups and saucers and biscuits.

'I must get back. I've a clinic this afternoon and patients to see this evening.'

Claudia, sitting beside her mother, watched Thomas, perfectly at ease, everything arranged as he had wished, calm and self-assured, listening to George explaining the difficulties of being a GP's wife. He made no attempt to mention his own work; she guessed that it was just as time-consuming and demanding.

She went out with him to his car presently, and he stood for a minute, looking down at her. 'I'll see you on Sunday evening. My mother and father will be with me in their own car. We'll put up at the Duck and Thistle.'

He took her two hands in his. 'Quite sure, Claudia?'

She said steadily, 'Yes, Thomas. It's a bit unusual, isn't it? Getting married like this. But if we're sure, and it's what we want, there's no point in mulling it over for months, is there? And I don't suppose that if we were engaged for a long time we'd see much of each other— I mean, get to know each other better—for you would be working and I'd be bogged down in plans for the wedding.'

'What a sensible girl you are, Claudia.' He bent and kissed her, a brief, friendly kiss, before getting into his car and driving away.

Back in the sitting room, her mother said, 'Darling, we're all so happy for you. He's just right for you and so handsome. You'll have a delightful life together. I can hardly believe it—there we were a few weeks ago, with not a penny piece between us and no roof over our heads, and look at us now. I'm here with George, and so very happy, and you'll be happy too with Thomas.'

She paused to look at Claudia. 'Clothes—you must have some new things...'

'I've told you about the dress and jacket, and the hat, and I've bought one or two other things. Enough to go on with. I expect I'll get some new clothes when we're in London. There hasn't been time, and Thomas knows that.' She added carefully, 'You see, there didn't seem much point in waiting—my job in the hospital wasn't quite what I thought it would be, and Thomas wanted me to leave as soon as possible.' She smiled suddenly. 'So did I.'

Mrs Willis started to say something, and then stopped. Instead she observed, 'I expect Thomas fell in love with you the first time you met...'

'It happens all the time,' said Claudia. 'Look at you and George.'

'Well, dear, for George, yes. But it took me a long time to discover that I loved him. And I dare say if it hadn't been for that awful Ramsay cousin, and us being turned out of the house, I might never have discovered how I felt.'

'What a good thing it happened that way, then. Though it was horrid, wasn't it? Do you hear or see anything of him and his wife?'

'No, dear. They keep themselves very much to themselves, and the village isn't friendly towards them.' Mrs Willis sighed happily. 'How nice that we don't have to think about them any more. Now, on Monday I thought that we would have a buffet lunch. Mrs Pratt is longing to prepare a feast for you. A pity that it is to be such a quiet wedding.' She glanced at Claudia. 'You don't mind?'

'No, Mother, I'm happy to do whatever Thomas wants. If we had decided to marry later on, we wouldn't have seen much of each other—he's busy all day most days. At least I shall see him when he comes home in the evenings.'

A remark which satisfied her mother, just as Claudia had meant it to.

Claudia woke early on Monday morning. It was still dark outside as she got out of bed, wrapped herself in her dressing gown and crept downstairs. The light was on in the kitchen and Mrs Pratt was there, carefully lifting tiny vol-au-vents from a baking sheet onto one of Dr Willis's best china dishes. Tombs was there too, sitting by the Aga, polishing wine glasses.

'No, no. Don't move,' said Claudia as he started to get up. 'I thought I'd make a cup of tea.'

Mrs Pratt beamed at her. 'You should still be in your bed, Miss Claudia. I dare say you're excited. It isn't every day a girl marries. The kettle's boiling, if you'd like to make tea...'

'We'll all have a cup. You're both coming to the church, aren't you?'

'Wouldn't miss it for all the tea in China, Miss Claudia,' said Tombs. 'Me and Mrs Pratt are that pleased. Took to the doctor the moment we set eyes on him, didn't we?'

Mrs Pratt, whipping something delicious in a bowl, agreed. 'A handsome pair you'll be—though it's to be hoped you won't let him see that old dressing gown, Miss Claudia. Warm and cosy it may have been at one time, but it's past its best...'

Claudia warmed the teapot and had a sudden moment of doubt. Surely Thomas would have realised that she had had no time to buy a lot of clothes? And would he mind anyway? She had gained the impression that her appearance wasn't something he found important. True, he had told her that she looked nice…

'I shall go shopping in London.' She turned to smile at Mrs Pratt. 'I'll leave this dressing gown behind!'

The three of them drank their tea in a friendly silence, and Rob, rousing from sleep in his basket, came to join them.

'I'll let him out and take the tea up as I go,' said Claudia.

'Begging your pardon, Miss Claudia,' said Tombs, at his most stately. 'You will do no such thing. That is a morning task for myself.'

'Oh, Tombs,' cried Claudia. 'I'm going to miss you and Mrs Pratt.'

She finished her tea and went to the garden door with Rob, who lumbered out into the garden. She stood watching him and looked at the sky, beginning to lighten. It had been a frosty night, and her breath drifted away in soft swirls. It was going to be a lovely winter's day. A good omen? She hoped so.

Rob came in then, making for the warmth of the Aga, and she went back to her room.

It was growing lighter by the minute. She went to the window, opened it wide and leaned out, breathing the cold air. At the other end of the village Thomas was sleeping—his parents too. They had come at teatime—Thomas in his Rolls Royce, his father driving a Daimler. She had seen them arrive from her bedroom window and hurried downstairs, her hair very tidy for once, wearing a dark green jersey dress which she had had for so long it had become quite fashionable again.

It was essential to make a good impression; Thomas's parents might live miles away, but they were bound to meet occasionally. She hadn't allowed herself to speculate about them, she'd only hoped that they would like her.

Thomas's mother had come in first, pausing to smile at Tombs, but before she reached Claudia, Thomas had been there, bending to kiss her cheek, putting an arm round her shoulder.

'This is Claudia, Mother—Father.' And they had both shaken her hand and kissed her warmly, so that her vague doubts had vanished.

Thomas's father was an elderly edition of his son, still very upright, grey-haired and handsome. His mother was almost as tall as Claudia, and still a beautiful woman, with a beauty she had allowed to age gradually, without excess make-up or tinted hair. Her face wrinkled in all the right places, and her hair was grey and simply dressed. But her eyes were still young—vivid blue and smiling. She was well dressed too, in an understated and slightly old-fashioned way. Claudia had liked her at once.

It had been easy after that first meeting. Her mother and George had joined them, and the evening had been pleasant. Neither of the Tait-Bullens had badgered her with questions; they had talked about the wedding in a soothing manner, remarked upon the charm of the village and told her something—but not much—of their own home. And she had had no chance to talk for more than a few moments to Thomas. Only as they had been leaving to go to the Duck and Thistle had he asked her kindly, 'Cold feet, Claudia?'

'Certainly not,' she had answered him indignantly, and then, looking into his face, seeing the casual friendliness in it, had added softly, 'No, I promise you, Thomas.'

Someone was coming down the lane from the village.

She withdrew her head and then poked it out again; in the dim light of dawn Thomas was coming through the open gate and up the short drive. He stopped under her window.

'Come for a walk?' he invited.

How could he have known that that was the very thing she most wanted to do?

'Five minutes,' said Claudia, and closed the window.

There were trousers and an old sweater in the cupboard; she put them on over her nightie, tied back her hair, cleaned her teeth and went down to the kitchen; her wellies were there, with socks stuffed inside them. Under Tombs's and Mrs Pratt's astonished gaze, she put them on, bundled on one of the coats hanging behind the kitchen door, blew them a kiss and went out into the garden round the house to where Thomas was waiting.

He took her arm and walked her briskly along the lane, away from the village. 'No gloves?' he asked, and took his own off and put them onto her cold hands. 'This isn't quite the usual behaviour of the bride and groom on their wedding day...'

'But it isn't a usual kind of wedding, is it?'

The lane petered out into a rough track, its rutted surface frost-bound, and as they walked Thomas began to talk—a nicely calculated jumble of odds and ends about his work, and information about his home, his friends... 'I hope you will like them—most of them are married...'

'Have you had any girlfriends? I'm not being nosy, but if I were to meet them I'd have to know who they are, wouldn't I?'

Mr Tait-Bullen didn't pause in his stride. He said briskly, 'Naturally I have been out and about with several woman acquaintances, but they have never been more than that, Claudia.'

'Have I annoyed you by asking? I don't expect to
know about your life, but I don't want to be taken un-
awares. Anyway, I don't suppose you've had much time
to fall in love.'

'I'm not sure if time is needed when one falls in love.
I imagine it happens in the blink of an eye. I can promise
you that I have had neither the inclination or the time. I
have always been too busy. But I shall enjoy being married to you; we shall be good friends and companions
and above all we like each other. Liking the person you
marry is as important as loving them.'

'I'm sure you're right,' said Claudia, 'although we
can't be quite certain, can we? I mean, you'd have to be
married to someone you loved and didn't like...'

They had been walking uphill; now they paused to
watch the first rays of a wintry sun creep over the
countryside. They stood and watched for a moment, and
Claudia said, 'Nice, isn't it?' She added slowly, 'That's
the only thing. I expect I'll miss this for a bit.'

'Yes, I can understand that. I thought we might look
around for a small house not too far from here, where
we can spend weekends. It's an easy run up to town.'

He had flung an arm round her, and she turned within
its comfort so that she could see his face. 'Oh, Thomas,
that would be lovely. But would you like that, too?'

'Very much. We will wait till after Christmas and then
go house-hunting. There are plenty of villages between
here and the M3.'

The sun was above the horizon now, and Claudia said
reluctantly, 'We'd better go back. We're not dressed for
the wedding, are we?'

Mr Tait-Bullen took a good look at her. 'No. I like
the hair, but you look all the wrong shape...'

'Well, I didn't stop to dress—only an old sweater and

trousers over my nightie. And I don't know whose coat this is—I took it from the back door.'

'And you still contrive to look beautiful,' he told her, and then turned her round smartly and marched her back.

He left her at the kitchen door, bending to kiss her quickly. 'Don't be late,' he said, and walked away as she opened the door.

'Your ma is in a fine state,' said Mrs Pratt. 'Miss Claudia, whatever possessed you to go gallivanting off like that? Looking like a scarecrow, too.'

Claudia flung her arms round her old friend's neck. 'It was lovely—a kind of ending and a beginning, if you see what I mean.' She skipped to the door and flew upstairs to shower, then put on her dressing gown again and went down to breakfast.

Mrs Willis submitted to her hug. 'Darling, you shouldn't have gone off like that—you and Thomas aren't supposed to see each other until you meet in church, and Mrs Pratt says you looked like a bag lady...'

Claudia helped herself to toast. 'It was lovely. We watched the sun come up. Mother, I'm so happy!'

And Mrs Willis, happy herself, leaned across the table and patted her daughter's arm. 'Oh, love, I do understand. So does George. He was called out just before you came downstairs—old Mrs Parson's grandson cut his arm on a bottle.'

'George will be back in time for the wedding?'

'Don't worry, dear, he will. It's only a matter of a few stitches.'

Claudia, casting a critical eye over her reflection, wished for a brief moment that it was white chiffon and yards of veiling and not the blue outfit she was looking at. She had dressed with care, taken pains with her face and her hair, and arranged the hat at the most becoming angle. She supposed that for a quiet wedding she looked all right.

Supposing it didn't work out well? Thomas was so sure that it would, and so was she, but that hadn't prevented last-minute doubts creeping in. Did all brides feel as she did? she wondered. Wondering if they were making the biggest mistake of their lives? Or was that because she was marrying Thomas after such a short time in which to know him?

She turned away from the mirror and went to look out of the window; she couldn't even see the Duck and Thistle from it, but it was only a few minutes' walk away. Was Thomas standing at his window as full of doubts as she was, perhaps wishing that he had never set eyes on her?

Her mother, coming into the room, broke into her thoughts. 'Darling, just look at this—Thomas doesn't know what you're wearing, so the flowers are white— isn't it gorgeous?'

The bouquet she was offering Claudia was truly bridal; white roses very faintly tinged with pink, lilies of the valley, hyacinth pips, orange blossom, little white tulips and miniature white narcissi nestling in a circle of green leaves. It made up for the lack of white chiffon; just looking at it made her feel like a bride.

A very quiet wedding, Thomas had said, but that hadn't prevented everyone in the village who could get to the church from going to see Claudia married. But they understood, sitting at the back of the church quietly so that Claudia and Thomas were unaware of them, knowing that they wanted a quiet wedding. Only as they left the church did she become aware of smiling faces and voices wishing them luck and happiness.

Back at George's house, they drank the champagne which Mr Tait-Bullen had thoughtfully provided, and presently sat down to an early lunch, waited upon by Tombs at his most majestic. Mrs Pratt, refusing to be discouraged by the brief notice she had had of the wedding, had sat up late and got up early in order to provide a feast worthy of the occasion.

Cheese soufflés, each in their own small ramekin, followed by salmon *en croûte*, watercress salad and potato straws, and, following that, Tombs carried in the wedding cake. Not quite in the traditional manner, perhaps— Mrs Pratt hadn't had time for that—but she had iced a fruit cake and ornamented it with silver leaves, searched for at length in the village shop, and arranged it on one of George's much prized Coalport plates, which he kept under lock and key.

'Nothing but the best for Miss Claudia,' Mrs Pratt had told him, standing over him while he took the plate from the glass cabinet where it was displayed.

It was a pleasant meal. No one made a speech, although they did drink the bride and groom's health, with Tombs and Mrs Pratt summoned from the kitchen, well pleased with their efforts, beaming at them from the door.

It was Thomas, refilling their glasses, who said, 'My wife and I thank you both for giving us such a delightful lunch; it has made our happy day even happier.'

They had coffee in the drawing room, and presently Thomas said, 'I think we should be going, Claudia.' He looked at George. 'We both thank you for making our wedding such a happy occasion. Once we are settled in we do hope that you will come and visit us.' He turned to his mother and said, 'And of course you and Father. But we shall be seeing you at Christmas.'

'We look forward to that, Thomas.'

It took quite a while saying goodbye to everyone. Thomas put the luggage in the car and then waited with no sign of impatience while Claudia went from one to the other. Tombs and Mrs Pratt had to be bidden goodbye, messages left for Jennie, and Rob hugged. But finally there were no more goodbyes to be said, and she went out to the car with Thomas and got in beside him. It wasn't until they had driven for a mile or two that she said in a small voice, 'It has all been so sudden...'

He touched her hand briefly. 'Don't worry, Claudia, I shan't hurry you. Think of us as being engaged, if that makes you feel happier...'

'Well, I dare say it would, but I won't. We're married, aren't we? Once I get used to that everything will be fine.' She added quickly, 'Don't think I'm regretting it; I'm not. I'm very happy—only a bit out of my depth.'

'You may have all the time in the world to find your feet. I have to work tomorrow, but on Wednesday I shall be home in the morning—time for us to talk.'

He was on the motorway now, driving fast through the already fading light.

'Cork will have tea for us and we shall have this evening together. I enjoyed our wedding, Claudia, and I hope you did too?'

'Oh, yes, I did. And the flowers—they were glorious. They made me forget that I was wearing an ordinary outfit. I felt as though I was in white chiffon and a veil— a real bride.'

'But you were a real bride, my dear. You looked beautiful...'

A remark which lifted her spirits, so that for the rest of the journey she was utterly happy.

CHAPTER FIVE

THOMAS'S description of his home in London had been vague; Claudia had gathered that he lived near his consulting rooms in a terraced house, and she had pictured a typical London house—solid, mid-Victorian, with rather a lot of red brickwork. And, since she knew very little of London, her visits having been confined to brief shopping expeditions and the occasional visit to a theatre, she'd visualised a busy road, noisy with traffic and not a tree in sight.

When Thomas stopped before his home, got out and opened her door, she got out too and stared around her. It was quite dark by now, but the street lighting was shining onto the elegant houses standing back from the tree-lined pavement. He took her arm and led her up the three steps to the door being held open, giving a glimpse of a softly lighted hall.

'Ah, Cork,' said Mr Tait-Bullen. 'Claudia, this is Cork, who looks after me so well and will doubtless do the same for you.' He put a hand on the other man's shoulder. 'My wife, Cork.'

Claudia offered a hand and smiled into the craggy face, and Cork allowed himself a pleased and relieved smile in return. A nice young lady, he saw at once, just right for his master.

'May I wish you both every happiness?' he observed solemnly. 'And I shall hope to give you as much satisfaction, madam, as the master.'

'Very nicely put,' said Mr Tait-Bullen, busy taking

Claudia's coat and gloves and tossing them and his own coat onto one of the chairs flanking the side table.

Cork allowed himself another smile. 'Tea will be brought to the drawing room in five minutes, sir.'

He melted away, and Thomas took Claudia's arm and led her through a door—one of three leading from the hall.

The room was large, with its windows overlooking the quiet street. There was an Adam fireplace, with two sofas and a maple and rosewood library table arranged before it, a Regency writing table under the window and a magnificent Chinese lacquer display cabinet facing the window. There were comfortable chairs too, upholstered in the same burgundy velvet as the curtains draping the window. And small lamp tables here and there, too, piled with books and magazines. A lovely room, restful and lived in.

Claudia felt instantly at home in it—a good augur for the future? she wondered, smiling at Cork, coming in with the tea tray. He didn't return the smile. She appeared to be a nice young lady, at first sight a suitable wife for his master, but time would tell, and he was a man who did nothing hastily. She might want to interfere in his kitchen...

Claudia had seen the prim set of his mouth. If Cork was anything like Tombs then she would need to tread carefully for a while. It had taken her quite a time to win over Tombs, but once she had he had become her firm friend and ally. She sat down in the chair Thomas had offered her and composedly poured their tea, as though she had been doing it for years.

Mr Tait-Bullen, leafing through his post, observed her from under his lids. He had known instinctively that she was the right wife for him: taking things in her stride, accepting each new challenge as it arose, fitting into his life without fuss. And he liked her; he liked her very much.

He considered himself beyond the age of falling in love, and he had no intention of doing so. His work was all-engrossing. The way of life that he had chosen suited him very well; he had no doubt that Claudia would accept that. They had similar tastes. She would be free to make her own friends, and whenever they had the time they would spend a day or so in the country. He must remember to do something about that...

Cork came back presently, removed the tea things and ushered her upstairs. The staircase was narrow, and curved against the end wall of the hall, and Claudia stopped to admire it. She ran a hand over its mahogany banisters, gleaming with polish. 'Lots of elbow grease,' she reflected out loud, and Cork gave her a respectful look.

'Nothing beats it, madam.' He allowed himself the ghost of a smile.

Her room was at the back of the house, overlooking a long, narrow garden. Even in winter it looked charming, with a tracery of leafless trees grouped here and there. Doubtless in the spring there would be crocuses and daffodils around them, and bright flowers in the summer.

She turned from the window and found Cork still standing at the door. 'The bathroom is through the door on the right, madam, and beyond that is the Professor's room. Tomorrow, if you wish, I will conduct you round the house.'

'Oh, please, Cork. And if you will tell me anything that I should know—advise me. You will know exactly how the—the Professor likes things done.'

'I trust so, madam.'

When she was alone she took stock of the room and could find no fault with it. The bed was a satinwood four-poster, curtained and covered with a gossamer-fine ivory silk patterned with forget-me-nots, and the bow-fronted chest was of the same wood. There was a satin-wood and mahogany mirror on the mahogany sofa table under the two windows, and a tallboy in exquisite mar-quetry. On either side of the bed were delicate little side tables, each with a china figure bearing a rose-coloured lamp. There was a wall cupboard too, she discovered, and beyond the further door a bathroom to be drooled over. She peeped round the door in the bathroom too: another bedroom, furnished more plainly, but with the same beautiful old pieces.

It was something she hadn't thought about; that Thomas had comfortable means had always been appar-ent, but this house of his was full of treasures. Had he inherited them? she wondered. Or did he collect old and valuable furniture as a hobby?

She went downstairs presently, determined to find out.

Thomas looked up from his letters as she went into the room. 'Is your room all right? Most of the furniture here was left to me by my grandmother, who had it from her husband's family—they had an enormous old house in Berkshire. I loved it when I went to stay with her as a boy, and I still do.'

'So do I, and it's just right for this house, isn't it?'

'I think so, and I'm glad you agree. This place isn't large but the period's right.'

'I was wondering—you know, while I was upstairs—if you collected old furniture or something like that?'

'No, but when we have found the house we like in the country we will spend time finding exactly the right furniture for it. I'm seldom free for any length of time, so it may take months.'

Lying in the four-poster, nicely drowsy, Claudia reviewed her wedding day. They had spent a happy evening together, talking like an old married couple, disagreeing pleasantly from time to time, discovering that they agreed about most things which mattered. Cork had served them with a splendid dinner—watercress soup, roast pheasant with all its trimmings, a dessert of his own devising—a concoction of ground almonds and whipped cream, angelica and crystallised fruit—and finally coffee in a very beautiful silver coffee pot, poured into paper-thin cups. They had drunk champagne, too, with Cork toasting them gravely and wishing them long life and happiness.

She had gone to bed quite happily. Wasn't there a song 'Getting to Know You'? That was what they were doing, wasn't it? Taking their time like two sensible people, but instead of getting engaged for a time before they married, they had married first.

'Let us give ourselves time to get to know and understand each other,' Thomas had said, and she had agreed. Life spread before her, undemanding and rather exciting. Tomorrow, she thought sleepily, she would go over the house with Cork, taking care not to encroach on his orderly life. She would wait for him to make the first suggestions as to what she should or should not do; later on, when he had accepted her, it would be for her to make suggestions...

Breakfast was at half past seven. When Thomas had suggested that she might like hers in bed, or later in the morning, she had told him that, no, she liked getting up early and would breakfast with him. She had seen his faint frown and hastened to add, 'Don't worry, I won't talk!'

In the morning she was as good as her word. Beyond a cheerful good morning she stayed silent, eating the scrambled eggs Cork put before her and following that with toast and marmalade. Thomas left before she had finished, dropping a hand on her shoulder as he went past her chair.

'I may be late home...'

'How late is late? Does Cork have a meal ready for you whatever time it is?'

'Yes. But I'll do my best to be here by eight o'clock. If I'm held up I'll phone, or get someone to do it for me.'

He had gone. She heard him speak to Cork in the hall before he went out to his car. She had finished breakfast when Cork came to clear the table.

'You will wish to see over the house, madam?'

'Yes, please, Cork. When it's convenient to you. I'm sure you have your day organised. I'd like to telephone my mother and write a letter or two, so will you let me know when you are ready? Does someone come in to give you a hand?'

'Mrs Rumbold comes each morning except Saturday and Sunday. A reliable, hardworking person, and entirely trustworthy. If it suits you, I will bring you coffee at ten o'clock, after which I shall be free to take you round the house.'

'Thank you, Cork. Ought I to meet Mrs Rumbold?'

'Certainly, if you wish, madam. I will bring her to you—she comes at nine o'clock.'

Claudia had a long and satisfying conversation with her mother, declaring herself to be entirely happy and promising a full description of the house later. She put

the phone down as Cork came in with Mrs Rumbold—
a stout lady with small dark eyes in a round face, a great
deal of hair, in a most unlikely shade of ebony, and a
wide smile.

Claudia got up and shook hands, and murmured suitably, and Mrs Rumbold's vast person quivered with
cheerful laughter.

'Lor' bless me, ma'am, it's a great treat to see another
female in the house. A bit of a surprise, but Mr Cork
tells me as 'ow you and the Professor 'as known each
other a while.'

Claudia smiled and said that, yes, indeed that was so.
Cork coughed, a signal for Mrs Rumbold to take her
departure, declaring that she'd do her best, same as always, and had never given Mr Cork cause to complain...

'I'm sure you haven't, Mrs Rumbold...'

She had her coffee presently, this time from a small
silver coffee pot and a much larger cup, delicately patterned with roses. It looked so fragile that Claudia was
in two minds as to whether to drink from it. But she did.

She went for a walk after lunch, finding her way round
the quiet streets, lined by similar houses, going to the
nearest main road to study the bus timetables. There
were no large stores close by, although she did find a
row of small shops tucked away behind an elegant row
of houses. The kind of shops she was used to—selling
wools and knitting needles and high-class green-
groceries, an antiquarian bookshop, a tiny tea shop—
very elegant—and at the end a dusty, rather shabby little
place selling small antiques and a variety of odds and
ends.

She spent some time looking in its window, and then
walked back, thinking about her morning. Cork had been
very helpful, but she felt he was still suspicious of her.

He had shown her every nook and cranny of the house, every cupboard... The house was bigger than she had thought at first: three storeys high and every room charmingly furnished. Cork had a room and bathroom behind the kitchen in the semi-basement, and she had no doubt that it was comfortably furnished too.

The kitchen was very much to her own taste; a cheerful red Aga, a vast old-fashioned dresser along one wall, filled with plates and dishes, a square wooden table in the centre of the room, around which were an assortment of comfortable, rather shabby chairs, and pots and saucepans neatly stacked on the shelves on the walls. There were checked curtains at the window and a thick rug before the Aga. It reminded her of Great-Uncle William's kitchen... She reached the front door and rang the bell, reminding herself that she must ask Thomas for a key.

Thomas didn't get home until almost eight o'clock. She saw that he was tired and, beyond answering his queries as to how she had spent her day, she forebore from chattering. They dined in a companionable silence, and, since it was by then getting late in the evening, she said that she was tired and would go to bed if he didn't mind. It had been the right thing to say, but she tried not to mind when she saw the relief on his face.

Still, he bade her goodnight and kissed her cheek, then reminded her that he was free in the morning and they would go shopping. 'I shall open an account for you at Harrods and Harvey Nichols, and arrange for an allowance to be paid into your bank. But tomorrow we will shop together.'

He took her first to Harrods the next morning, accompanying her to the fashion floor, telling her to buy whatever she liked and making himself comfortable in one of the easy chairs scattered around.

'You mean a dress and coat, and things like that?' asked Claudia. 'How much may I spend?'

'One dress will hardly do. Buy several—and certainly a winter coat and anything else you like. Don't look at the price tags, Claudia.' He smiled at her. 'Buy all you need for the next few weeks; we shall be going out a good deal, I have no doubt...'

'Dinner dresses,' breathed Claudia, and her eyes sparkled.

'Certainly, and a couple of dresses for dancing—the hospital ball and so on. And something tweedy for the lakes. I shall take you walking.'

'You don't mind waiting here?'

'Not in the least. Come and show me what you buy from time to time, if you like.'

So Claudia, guided by a majestic saleslady in black crêpe, went shopping in earnest. She had had nothing new for some time, and her present wardrobe was sparse in the extreme, but that didn't prevent her from knowing exactly what she needed to buy.

A beautifully tailored winter coat in dark green, a tweed skirt with a matching soft leather jacket, a twinset in cashmere, peat-brown, a jersey dress in soft blue and another in dove-grey, and, at the sales lady's suggestion, a handful of silk blouses and another cardigan. She had shown most of these to a patient Mr Tait-Bullen, then gone with him to the restaurant for a cup of coffee before embarking on the choosing of a crêpe dress in old gold, and another in a green patterned silk jersey. She would have bought a little black dress, but when she mentioned her intention to Thomas he begged her not to. 'They're not for you,' he told her. 'Get something with a waist and a wide skirt.'

Which wasn't much to go by. Anxious to please him, she spent some time looking for such a garment, and found it at last. Blue again—a smoky blue—with long sleeves and a modest neckline, and a tucked bodice cinched in at the waist by an embroidered belt, the skirt was several layers of chiffon, and it showed off her splendid figure. She paraded before him in it and saw that he approved.

'Would you like me to stop now?' she asked him.

'No. No. Let us by all means get the basics. What else do you need?'

'Well, evening dresses. I won't be long…'

She knew what suited her and she didn't dither, although there was a magnificent black taffeta she longed to own… She chose instead a russet taffeta with a tucked bodice, shoestring shoulder straps and a wide skirt which rustled delightfully as she walked. And a honey-coloured crêpe, very simple in cut.

'I've bought masses of clothes,' she told Thomas finally. 'I do hope….'

'We'll have lunch, and, if you haven't made me bankrupt, we will go to Harvey Nichols.'

'But I've bought masses of stuff.'

'Undies, dressing gowns, shoes, boots, a Burberry—a hat for church on Christmas Day?'

She stared up at him with wide eyes. 'You think of everything.'

'No, my dear, but you forget I have sisters, and I have from time to time accompanied them on shopping expeditions.'

'Oh, well, if you don't mind.'

'No, I don't mind,' said Mr Tait-Bullen, and thought how very pretty she looked.

They lunched at Harvey Nichols, in the basement bar-restaurant because Claudia declared that she was too full of excitement to eat much. All the same, gently urged on by Thomas, she managed grilled salmon and a salad, and apple tart, and, thus fortified, spent the next hour or so adding to her wardrobe. Having approved of the Burberry, boots, and shoes, Thomas left her in the undies department.

'I'll look around for presents for the family,' he told her, 'on the ground floor.' He glanced at his watch. 'An hour? I'll be waiting by the main entrance.' He smiled down at her happy face. 'Don't hurry.'

She lost herself in the delights of the lingerie department, but she remembered that he had said an hour. Laden with carrier bags, she went punctually to the ground floor and found him waiting.

He looked at the bags. 'They can be delivered with the other things,' he suggested.

She shook her head. 'I can't bear to part with them,' she told him seriously. 'You have no idea how lovely...'

'Shall we go home for tea?' he asked in a matter-of-fact way, which stopped her short.

They had their tea, and then an hour or so sitting together talking about nothing in particular. There would be more Christmas presents to buy, he warned her. And would she like to go to Little Planting before Christmas?

'I can spare a Sunday, if you would like that. And don't forget the hospital ball next week. You will be bound to get any number of invitations for us both from the people we meet there. I rely on you to deal with them. There is a certain amount of hospital social life, and you will probably be roped in for some charity or other. Don't take on too much…'

They were halfway through dinner when he was called away. He went quickly, warning her that he might be late back.

As he went he dropped a kiss on her cheek. 'I enjoyed our day together,' he told her.

'Me too. Only I've spent an awful lot of your money…'

'Our money,' he said quietly. 'It was a great pleasure.'

She sat in the drawing room that evening, leafing through magazines, thinking about her delightful day. Thomas had been a splendid companion too. Patient, and interested in what she had bought. Of course, she quite understood that as the wife of a well-known cardiologist she needed to be well turned out—he wouldn't want her to meet any of his friends and colleagues wearing the shabby tweeds and woollies she had always worn at Little Planting.

She got up and took a look at herself in the Georgian giltwood mirror. Perhaps she should have her hair cut and styled? Go to a beauty parlour and learn how to apply make-up? She tended to forget anything but lipstick; there had seemed no point in it when she lived with Great-Uncle William. On the sparse occasions when she'd gone out to dinner she had dashed powder over her nose, added lipstick and done her best with her hands, so often grubby from gardening. She would remedy this, she promised herself, so that Thomas need never feel ashamed of her.

The long case clock in the hall had struck eleven, and he still wasn't back. She went to the kitchen and found Cork sitting there, reading the evening paper.

She said quickly, 'No, no. Don't get up, Cork. I think

I'll go to bed. Do you wait up or does the Professor let himself in? And does he need anything? A drink? Or sandwiches?'

'I wait up, madam. There is coffee, and there are sandwiches if he should require them. I'm sure he would wish you to take your normal rest.'

'Yes, well...I'll go to bed, then. Thank you, Cork.'

'Thank you, madam, and goodnight.'

He held the door for her and didn't return her smile. She went up to her room, still not sure if he approved of her or not. She must have been a surprise to him, and doubtless he wondered if she was going to interfere. She didn't intend to; perhaps she'd do the flowers, discuss the food with him, and then later on, when he had accepted her, he might allow her into the kitchen.

Thomas was already at breakfast when she went down in the morning. He looked as he always did, immaculate in his sober grey suit and silk tie, but there were lines in his face...

She wished him good morning. 'When did you get home?' she asked.

'Round about one o'clock. I didn't disturb you?'

'No, no. Do you often get called out? I thought specialists and consultants could more or less please themselves.'

Mr Tait-Bullen looked surprised. 'We're just the same as any other medical man. We go when and where we're needed.'

'And you are going to the hospital this morning?'

'No, first to one of the private hospitals. I operated there a couple of days ago, and I must visit my patient there first. Then to the hospital, and a clinic after lunch, and then private patients at my consulting rooms.'

'Will you come home for lunch?'

He shook his head. 'I'm afraid not. I may be back in time for tea, though.' He glanced at her. 'You'll be all right?'

'Yes…'

'I should have warned you that I'm away a good deal.'

He left the house presently, and, since Cork informed her that it was Mrs Rumbold's day for turning out the drawing room, she guessed quite rightly, that they would like her out of the house.

'I thought I'd explore a bit,' she told him. 'Hyde Park and perhaps Kensington Gardens…'

'A pleasant walk, madam. Lunch at one o'clock?'

'Yes, please. Something on a tray will do.'

She had put on the tweed skirt and one of the silk shirts, and, since it was drizzling with a chilly wind, she donned the Burberry and the boots. The Burberry had a little matching hat, which she crammed onto her hair with no regard to her appearance, so that copper strands escaped. She took her new shoulder bag, her expensive leather gloves, bade Cork goodbye and left the house.

There weren't many people about as she made her way to Marble Arch. Cork, that paragon of servants, had thoughtfully provided her with a small street map, and it wasn't until she reached Marble Arch that there was much traffic and the first sight of Christmas shoppers.

She crossed the road into the park, following the Serpentine, enjoying the quiet emptiness, for there was scarcely anyone else to be seen. She was halfway to Rennie's Bridge, which would lead her to Kensington Gardens, when she saw a very small dog sitting under the bushes some yards from the path. He didn't bark, nor did he take any notice of her, and she walked on, supposing that its owner was somewhere nearby. But an hour later, as she came back the same way, he was still there.

There was no one in sight; she crossed the grass and bent down to take a closer look.

It was a very small dog indeed—a puppy, pitifully thin and shivering with cold. It made no sound as Claudia touched his matted coat with a gentle hand; it only looked at her with terrified eyes, cringing away from her. He was tied by a thin rope to a thicket behind him, and she could see that the rope was tight around his throat. If he'd tried to run away he would have choked.

She opened her bag, found the small folded scissors she always carried with her and began to saw through the rope. It took time, but the puppy didn't move, and when at last he was free she scooped him up and tucked him into the front of her Burberry, where he shivered and shook but made no effort to escape.

'You poor little scrap,' said Claudia. 'You're coming home with me, and I'll make sure that you're never frightened nor hungry again.'

It was only as she reached the house that she wondered what Thomas would say—or Cork!

He had seen her coming along the street and had the door open before she had a chance to get out her key.

She didn't beat about the bush. 'Cork, I found this tiny dog tied to a tree in Hyde Park. He's starving and cold...'

Cork peered at the small creature. 'The Professor has said on various occasions that he intended to get a dog, madam. Perhaps, a box with an old blanket by the Aga?'

'Oh, Cork, may he stay just until he's warm? And I thought a little warm milk... I'll have him as soon as I've got my things off.'

'If I might suggest, madam, you allow him to rest quietly for a period while you have lunch. By then we shall be able to see if he is recovering.'

So the puppy was settled in a cardboard box and covered warmly, and Claudia fed him with warm milk. Although he cringed still, he looked less terrified.

He was asleep when she went to fetch him after lunch.

'Thank you for having him in the kitchen, Cork, I won't let him bother you.'

'I have no doubt that when he is feeling more himself he will be a nice little dog. I'm partial to dogs, madam.'

Claudia beamed at him. 'Oh, are you, Cork? So am I.'

She took the little beast with her to the sitting room beside Thomas's study—a charming little room, where she chose to sit and have her meals when Thomas was away from home—and he fell asleep by the warmth of the fire, twitching and whimpering in his sleep. And when Cork brought her tea tray he handed her a small jug. 'Egg and milk, madam,' he explained. 'Perhaps a few spoonfuls from time to time...'

They inspected the sleeping puppy and decided that he looked a little better.

'As soon as I dare, I'll clean him up a bit,' said Claudia. 'He's stopped shivering...'

She went to her room presently, and changed her blouse and skirt for one of the jersey dresses, not bothering overmuch about her face and hair. She was feeding the puppy, kneeling by the box, rather untidy about the head, when Thomas came quietly to join her.

She scrambled to her feet when she saw him. 'Thomas, I'm so glad you're home. Come and see what I found this morning...' She paused while Cork placed a tea tray on the rent table by the easy chair where Mr

Tait-Bullen often sat. 'I'll pour your tea. Have you had a busy day?'

He could see that for the moment his day would have to take second place to whatever it was in the box which had given her eyes such a sparkle and her cheeks such a fine colour.

'And what did you find?' He went over to the box and got down on his hunkers to take a better look.

'Cork says you always wanted a dog...'

Mr Tait-Bullen choked back a laugh. 'Oh, indeed I have.' He put a gentle finger on the skinny little body. 'Lost? Starved? Probably ill-treated. Where did you find him?'

'Sit down and drink your tea and I'll tell you. Then you can examine him, can't you?'

He drank his tea and ate the toast she offered him, and listened without interrupting. 'And Cork has been marvellous. I thought he would mind—I mean, a grubby little dog in this lovely house—'

'Our house,' he interrupted her gently.

'Well, of course it is, but you know what I mean, don't you? Please may we keep him? I don't know what kind of a dog he is, but I dare say he'll be handsome when he's older.'

Mr Tait-Bullen studied the puppy thoughtfully. 'There is always that possibility,' he agreed. 'Let's have a look at him.'

Claudia was surprised to see that the puppy accepted Thomas's gentle hands feeling his poor, bony frame, with no more than the whisper of a whine.

'Starved and kicked around, but I can't feel any broken bones. I'm on nodding terms with the local vet; I'll get him to come round and take a look.'

'May we keep him? You don't mind?'

'No, I don't mind. Cork was right. I have often said that I would like a dog.' He didn't add that the dog he had had in mind was a thoroughbred Labrador.

They dined presently, and tended to the puppy's needs, and later that evening the vet came. He was a youngish, thickset man, with a great deal of black hair and a face one could trust.

'Thomas, what's all this about a dog? Where did you get it?'

'Come and meet my wife. It was she who found the creature.'

The two men crossed the hall to the sitting room, where Claudia had gone to feed the puppy.

The vet shook hands. He had heard about Tait-Bullen's unexpected marriage, and, glancing at Claudia, he considered him to be a lucky fellow. Beautiful and charming—nice voice too.

He said out loud, 'I must get Alice—my wife—to call on you. Now, where's this dog?'

He took his time going over the puppy's small frame. 'No bones broken. Several swellings, though—he's been kicked. And just look at these paws—he's been tied up somewhere and tried to escape. Poor little beast.'

'Any idea what breed?' said Mr Tait-Bullen.

'Take your pick. He'll never be a large dog, nor perhaps a handsome one, but I guarantee he'll be a faithful companion to you both. I'll give him a couple of jabs while I'm here. As to food and exercise…'

He outlined suitable treatment. 'And a run in the garden is all he'll need for several weeks—that and frequent small meals.' He looked at Claudia. 'You will be busy, Mrs Tait-Bullen.'

'I've time enough to look after him, and I shall enjoy it. You'll have a cup of coffee?'

He stayed for a while, idly chatting, and presently
Thomas went with him to the door. 'You've a charming
wife, Thomas. You must come to dinner one evening.'

'We'll be delighted.'

He went back to the sitting room, where Claudia was
kneeling by the puppy's box. She looked up as he went
in. 'Thomas, thank you. Perhaps he's not the kind of
dog you wanted, but he'll be such fun to have.'

Mr Tait-Bullen contemplated the skinny creature, sitting up now and no longer cowering, knowing that he
was among friends. Under the dirt and mud his coat was
black. His ears were far too large for his small foxy face,
and he had a long, thin tail of which any rat would have
been proud.

'I have no doubt that he will grow into the most unusual type,' he observed gravely.

'That's what I thought,' said Claudia happily. 'I like
the vet. Are all your friends as nice?'

'I hope you will think so. You will meet a good many
of them at the ball.' He went to sit in his chair, stretching
his long legs to the fire. 'I'm sure you have a grand gown
to wear among your purchases, or would you like to look
for something else?'

'I have a gown. It's not grand, but I think it's suitable
for your wife, if you see what I mean?'

'I trust your judgement, Claudia. You have excellent
taste.'

Claudia went to bed with the pleasant feeling that it
had been a happy day; they got on so well together, she
reflected, and there was so much to talk about, so much
that they intended to do together. Every day, she was
discovering, she was finding out something else about
Thomas that she liked; she hoped that he felt the same

about her. She curled up and closed her eyes. Tomorrow was another day; she wondered what it would bring.

Fortunately for her peace of mind she wasn't to know *who* it would bring!

CHAPTER SIX

THE day began well. Thomas had no need to leave the house until nine o'clock, so they had leisure to clean up the puppy, anoint his battered little paws and brush his coat while he lay on Claudia's lap.

'What shall we call him?' she asked. 'A nice English name, since I found him in Hyde Park.'

'Since you found him you must choose his name.'

'Yes, well...' She thought for a moment. 'Harvey—that's easy to say, isn't it?'

Harvey cocked an ungainly ear; he was beginning to look more like a dog every minute.

Mr Tait-Bullen went presently, promising that he would be back for tea unless some emergency turned up.

'Oh, good,' said Claudia, with such transparent pleasure that he turned to look at her. She met his gaze with a look of faint enquiry. 'You look surprised. But teatime is one of the nicest parts of the day, isn't it? You can tell me what you've been doing and I'll listen...'

Mr Tait-Bullen discovered to his surprise that the idea appealed to him.

At four o'clock Cork arranged the tea things on a small table in the drawing room, and, since Mr Tait-Bullen had phoned to say that he would be home shortly after half past four, Claudia carried Harvey in his box from the sitting room and set it near the open fire. She had been out walking again, and was still in the tweed skirt and a blouse, but she had tidied her hair and powdered her nose and put on a pair of elegant kid slippers. She was sitting admiring them when Thomas came in.

He crossed the room and dropped a quick kiss on her cheek. 'How very cosy it is here. Cork's bringing the tea.'

He sat down opposite her. 'You have had a happy day? Harvey is doing well?'

'He's better. Look at him, Thomas. He's almost like a normal puppy.'

Harvey took this as a compliment and waved his tail.

'You don't mind him being in here? I don't think he'll get out of his box.'

'I don't imagine he could do much harm even if he did. He certainly looks more like a dog.' Thomas stretched an arm and tickled Harvey behind one ear. 'I must let John know how he's getting on. I dare say he'll want to see him again.'

Cork brought in the tea then, and buttered muffins in a dish, a fruit cake and a plate of paper-thin sandwiches. He arranged everything just so, and stood back to admire his handiwork.

Claudia said, 'Thank you, Cork, it all looks delicious. I hope you're going to have your own tea now?'

'Thank you, madam, yes. Dinner at the usual hour? You won't be going out again, sir?'

'I hope not, Cork.' And, as Cork slid through the door, Thomas added, 'I've a mass of paperwork to sort out. A quiet evening at home to get that done will be delightful.'

Claudia, pouring tea, agreed placidly. If she had been looking forward to an evening in his company, she didn't utter the thought aloud.

They were inspecting the fruit cake when the front doorbell was rung. And, before either of them had time to speak, Cork opened the door and stood aside to let someone in.

Mr Tait-Bullen got to his feet, his face expressionless, and his pleasant, 'Why, Honor, how nice to see you,' giving nothing away of his feelings.

Claudia stood up too, recognising in an instant that here was someone she wasn't going to like and who wasn't going to like her. But she smiled, a bright social smile, and then looked enquiringly at Thomas.

'My dear, let me introduce Honor Thompson. Honor, my wife, Claudia.'

Claudia offered a hand. 'Do sit down and have a cup of tea. I'll get Cork to bring a fresh pot...'

Honor sat on the sofa facing the fire, throwing off her coat to reveal a black dress—very short, very smart and undoubtedly very expensive. It showed off her long legs and her very slim body.

No shape at all, thought Claudia, and wondered if Thomas admired women who looked like beanpoles. She was suddenly aware of her own curves, and busied herself with the fresh tea Cork had brought in, listening with half an ear to Honor's rather loud voice complaining that she had had no idea that Thomas was getting married and why hadn't he told her. 'You must have known what a shock it would be to me.'

She glanced at Claudia, who handed her a cup and saucer. 'I expect you and Thomas are very old friends,' Claudia remarked. 'But, you see, we didn't tell anyone except our families. It was a very quiet wedding.'

'Well, I for one shan't forgive you easily, Thomas,' said Honor, and she leaned forward to lay a hand on his arm.

Mr Tait-Bullen got up and put his cup and saucer on the table without answering her, and she flushed angrily.

'Of course, I don't suppose you know much about Thomas. You can't have known each other long.' She gave Claudia a sly look.

'Long enough to know that we wanted to be married,' said Claudia, in a matter-of-fact voice which robbed the question of drama. 'You live in London?'

'Of course. Where else is there?'

'You don't care to travel?' asked Claudia guilelessly. 'I mean, around England? Perhaps all your friends live here?'

'I hate the country. I adore the theatre and dining out and dancing.' She gave a little trill of laughter. 'I can see that Thomas will have to change his ways now that he is a married man.'

'I expect most men do,' said Claudia cheerfully. 'And I don't suppose they mind or they wouldn't marry, would they?' She smiled at Thomas. 'Don't you agree, Thomas?'

'Wholeheartedly. Honor, take a look at our addition to the household.'

He bent and picked up Harvey, tucked him under an arm and went over to where Honor was sitting.

She eyed Harvey with dislike. 'You aren't serious? It's a horrid little stray. He must be filthy, and he's hideously ugly...'

'He's a brave little dog. We call him Harvey—he'll probably grow into something quite splendid. He's still rather grubby, but he's been ill-treated—look at this sore on his shoulder, and under his paws...'

Honor shrank back. 'Don't come any nearer with the nasty little brute...' She stood up. 'I must go. I'm going out this evening.' She turned a cold eye on Claudia. 'Nice meeting you, Claudia. I dare say we shall see each other around—that is, if you go out much socially.'

She didn't shake hands, and she didn't shake hands with Thomas either, since he was still holding Harvey. She reached the door as Cork, summoned by the bell-push by the fireplace, opened it and ushered her out.

It wasn't until he had returned and carried away the tea tray that Claudia said, 'I hope you're grateful that I married you. She would have eaten you alive in a couple of years. Are all your girl friends like that?'

Mr Tait-Bullen had gone back to his chair with Harvey curled up on his knee. He had expected a reproachful comment, or at least coolness and hurt looks, and he was taken aback by Claudia's cheerful question. Taken aback and, he had to admit, amused.

'I only now begin to realise what a treasure I have married. I am indeed grateful that you are my wife; calm, good sense and not a single sulky look. I can assure you that I have never had any intention of marrying Honor, although I suspect that she had the intention of marrying me. And I have had no girlfriends. Oh, I have taken Honor out from time to time, and other women too, but on a strictly platonic basis. I have not been in love for a very long time. If that were so, I would have told you.'

'Oh, my goodness, I didn't mean to pry. It's none of my business. All the same, I'm glad that it's me you married.'

'And so am I. Now, let us forget the woman and talk about other things which matter. I can be free next Sunday; shall we go down to Little Planting? Will your mother and George be home?'

'Yes, they only went away for a few days because they want to spend Christmas at home, and Mother enjoys all the preparations, you know—the tree and paper chains and holly and presents. She always managed to

make it a lovely time when we lived with Great-Uncle
William.'

'Then we will go, and take Harvey with us. Do you
want to shop for presents?'

'I could go tomorrow...and what about your family?
Should we not buy more presents for them?'

'I can't spare the time; if I give you a list, will you
do your best for us both?'

It was the kind of question that required nothing more
than a meek answer.

She went shopping the next morning; Thomas had left
the house early, and she found no one when she went
down to breakfast, but by her plate was a list of names
scrawled in his unreadable writing. A long list, starting
with his mother and ending with someone called
Maggie, with brackets beside her name requesting warm
slippers, size six! His father wasn't mentioned—presumably he bought that present himself. She added Cork's
name, and Mrs Rumbold's. Probably Thomas gave them
money, but a personal gift was always nice to have...

She found a cashmere stole for her mother-in-law, silk
scarves for his sisters, and a small leather case contain-
ing razor, hairbrush and a variety of small necessities
which a man might need when travelling. And then she
decided that scarves weren't enough for his sisters; she
added a small silver photo frame and a little enamelled
box. There were nephews and nieces too; she spent a
happy hour in the toy department of Harrods.

Thomas got home in the early evening, and she saw
at once that for the moment at least he had no wish to
look at what she had bought. He had greeted her in his
usual manner, given her a drink, poured one for himself
and gone to sit in his chair. Harvey had climbed out of

his box and wriggled his way on to his knee, and Thomas now stroked the small creature gently.

'You have had a pleasant day?' he asked presently.

'Yes, thank you. But you don't want to hear about it for the moment, do you? Do you want to talk about your day? I dare say I won't understand the half of it, but I'll be a pair of ears.'

He laughed then. 'Claudia, you are so understanding. It is as if we had been married for years—you are such a comfortable woman to come home to. And at the end of the day sometimes a pair of ears is what I most want.'

He began to talk: a difficult diagnosis, a long list in Theatre, a post-operative patient who wasn't progressing as well as he should, and always a backlog of patients who needed his skill.

Claudia listened to every word. There was quite a bit she didn't understand, but that didn't matter; she was intelligent enough to have a good idea as to his working day.

Presently she asked, 'Do you have a team working with you?'

'Yes, a splendid one. My senior registrar is a most dependable man, and I have two junior registrars and a couple of young surgeons—you'll meet them all at the ball. And a splendid theatre sister too.'

Claudia felt a faint flicker of something which she didn't recognise as jealousy. All she knew was that she felt regret that *she* couldn't be his theatre sister, working beside him.

Thomas smiled across at her. 'Have I bored you? You must tell me if I do.'

'No, I like to know something of your work. I'm really interested.'

Cork came to tell them then that dinner was on the

table and Thomas said, 'You must tell me what you have bought...'

She spent the next day shopping for her mother and George, and Tombs, Mrs Pratt and Jennie. It was nice having enough money to choose presents without having to bother too much about their price. Thomas had given her a very generous allowance, and told her carelessly not to worry if she spent too much, but she reminded herself that she hadn't married him for his money. Indeed, she admitted, she would have married him if he were penniless. The thought surprised her, and left her feeling disquieted.

The day after that was the hospital ball. Anxious to present as pleasing a picture as possible, Claudia spent most of the afternoon doing her nails, washing her hair, and experimenting with make-up. But by teatime she had decided that her usual dash of powder and lipstick would do. As for her hair, after a tiring hour pinning it into a variety of elaborate styles, she decided to twist it into a chignon—a simple style which suited her lovely face and which required no fuss. She suspected that Thomas would dislike it if she were to fidget about her appearance.

He had expected to be home early, but Cork had carried away the tea things and there was no sign of him. They had planned to have a light meal before going to the ball, and when she heard the clock strike seven she went along to the kitchen with Harvey trotting beside her.

'Cork, what is best to be done? We are to leave here by half past eight, and the Professor will want time to change. Would it be a good idea if you served a meal in the sitting room? We were going to have grilled soles, weren't we? Could they be saved for tomorrow? And could you give us soup and an omelette? Then whatever time he comes in we could eat when he is ready?'

'I have been thinking along those lines, madam: a plain omelette with a small salad, and I have prepared a sustaining soup with fresh-baked rolls.'

'Cork, that will be simply splendid. I'm going up to dress…'

Thomas came home half an hour later and Claudia, fresh from her bath and ready save for getting into her dress, wrapped her dressing gown round her and went down to meet him.

He looked tired after his long day, but he said cheerfully, 'Hello—did you begin to think I wasn't coming home?'

'Well, we were getting a bit anxious.' He hadn't kissed her, but she told herself that it didn't matter a bit. 'Would you like a meal at once, or do you want to change first?'

'I see that you aren't dressed yet.' He eyed her pretty pink quilted dressing gown. 'Shall we eat now?'

'Cork has a meal ready for us; we're having it in the sitting room. How well he looks after you, Thomas.'

He looked at her sharply. 'And you, too?'

'Heavens, yes! He's a treasure.' She led the way into the sitting room, scooping up Harvey as they went. He was still a somewhat battered little animal, but now that he found himself among friends, he was full of a desire to please.

Cork offered the soup, and presently the omelette, looking gratified when Thomas observed that it was exactly the meal he needed. Cork, having overheard Claudia's praise of him, murmured that it was madam who had suggested it. It was an unusually generous remark on his part, but he was becoming aware that

Claudia had no intention of ousting him from his position in the household. In fact, he was beginning to like her.

The meal eaten, they went away to dress, and half an hour later met again in the drawing room. Claudia, in the cream chiffon, wasn't sure if Thomas would find it grand enough, but she need not have worried.

He watched her cross the room. 'Delightful, Claudia. Exactly right. You look charming.' He took a box from the table beside him. 'Will you wear these?' he asked. 'I think they will go very well with the dress.'

He offered pearls, a double row with a diamond clasp, and to go with them earrings, pearl drops set in a delicate network of diamonds.

'My goodness,' said Claudia, 'they're magnificent, Thomas.' She touched the pearls with a gentle finger. 'I'm almost afraid to wear them.' She smiled at him. 'Thank you very much.'

She stretched up and kissed his cheek, and he took the necklace from her and fastened it round her throat.

'My grandmother left them to me with the advice that they should be given to my wife when I married.'

'She must have loved you,' said Claudia, and swallowed disappointment; they weren't a present from Thomas—not something he had wanted to buy for her, to give her as a present; he was merely carrying out his grandmother's wishes.

She said rather too brightly, 'I'm ready if you want to leave now.'

He gave her a thoughtful look, which she met with an equally bright smile. He looked distinguished in his black tie; the formal suit, cut by a master tailor, emphasised his height and size. He was a handsome man, she reflected, who ignored his good looks and had not an ounce of conceit. He was high-handed at times, perhaps, and capable of a fine rage, she suspected, but, like so many large men, gentle.

Cork, with Harvey tucked under an arm, saw them from the house, and it was only when they were driving through the quiet streets towards the busy heart of the city that Claudia felt the first pangs of nervousness.

'I don't know anyone...'

She felt his large, comforting hand on her knee for a moment. 'Don't worry, my dear, you will soon have more friends and acquaintances than you can imagine.'

'Oh—are you very well known, Thomas?'

'Well, I do visit a number of hospitals, and have done for some years now.'

He turned the car into the hospital forecourt, parked and helped her out.

He nodded to one of the porters standing at the entrance, and one of them got into the car and drove it away as they went in.

After that Claudia found herself in a sort of dream world. Thomas led her from one hospital dignitary to the other, a hand under her elbow guiding her, and when the formalities were over he took her onto the dance floor. He danced well, in an unspectacular way, guiding her effortlessly through the crowded hall, talking casually from time to time, putting her at her ease so that presently she found herself dancing with a variety of partners and enjoying herself.

From time to time she glimpsed him dancing, partnering his colleagues' wives, she supposed, slightly older women, well dressed and self-assured, but once or twice she saw that he was dancing with pretty girls, who laughed up into his face as though they had known him for years...

She was about to take to the floor with a stout, bearded man, whom she vaguely remembered having been introduced to, when Thomas slipped a hand under her elbow.

'The supper dance,' he observed mildly. 'You don't mind, Harry, if I claim my wife?'

The bearded man laughed. 'It wouldn't make a scrap of difference if I did, Thomas, but I shall lie in wait for you, Mrs Tait-Bullen!'

'Who was that?' asked Claudia, accepting a plate of vol-au-vents and a glass of wine. 'I've met him, haven't I?'

'Yes, he's the consultant pathologist and an old friend.' He smiled. 'You're enjoying yourself? I've been showered with compliments about my bride.'

She went pink. 'Oh, have you? People are very kind.'

'I have been told how beautiful you are—and you are, Claudia, that dress is exactly right.'

Somehow that last bit spoilt the compliment.

'You have been dancing with some very pretty girls. Of course, you must know all the nurses.'

He fetched her a little dish of ice cream before he replied.

'Not quite all. You see, I meet only ward sisters and staff nurses, and then our conversation is purely professional, but once a year at this ball the senior staff dance with those of the nursing staff they work with on the wards or in Theatre or the clinics. I don't know who started the idea, but the custom is handed down from one generation of doctors to the next.'

A remark which she found reassuring.

It was well past midnight when they got back home. Cork had left hot chocolate on the Aga, and they sat drinking it while Harvey snoozed in his basket.

'A very pleasant evening,' observed Mr Tait-Bullen, 'and you have won all hearts, Claudia.'

'It's nice of you to say so, but it's only because I'm a nine-days wonder.'

He laughed. 'What a matter-of-fact girl you are.' He took her mug from her. 'And a sleepy one, too. I must leave the house by seven o'clock, so don't get up until you have had your sleep. I should be home for tea.'

'Oh, good.' She yawned, and rubbed her eyes like a child. 'It was a lovely evening, and it was lovely to dance.'

He got up and hauled her gently from her chair. 'Indeed it was.'

He opened the door and gave her a gentle shove. 'Off to bed, and sleep well.'

She hesitated a moment, but he held the door open, smiling a little, so she wished him goodnight and took herself off to bed, feeling vaguely unhappy.

She woke late, and when she went downstairs Cork was waiting for her with Harvey scampering at his heels.

'You slept well, madam? I have set breakfast in the sitting room by the fire. A most inclement day, I'm afraid. I am to tell you from the Professor not to venture too far in this weather.'

Claudia peeped out of the window. Indeed, it looked horrid outside—dull and grey with an unremitting drizzle.

'It looks awful, Cork, but Harvey must have his run...'

'Perhaps a brisk turn in the garden, madam. There is always the chance that the weather will improve.'

'Well, I hope it does, for we are going to Little Planting on Sunday. We'll take Harvey with us.' She poured her coffee. 'Cork, you do have a day off each week, don't you?'

'I have two half-days, madam, and such free time as I can arrange without upset to the running of the house.'

He sounded cagey, and she added hastily, 'I'm sure you have it all worked out, Cork. But I just thought that it would be a chance for you to have a day to yourself while we are out.'

'Thank you, madam. I shall avail myself of your offer...'

'I expect that you have family and friends to visit?'

'Indeed, I have. At what time will you be leaving on Sunday, madam?'

'Quite early, I believe, and we shan't be back here until after tea.'

She finished her breakfast and spent the morning tying up presents, considerably hampered by Harvey. When, after lunch, the drizzle ceased, she got into her mac, tied Harvey into his waterproof jacket, and led him out for a quick walk. On the way home she stopped to look in the windows of the little shops she had found. The wool shop had a pretty knitting pattern in the window, with a basket of wools every colour of the rainbow. She already had a present for her mother, but there was no reason why she shouldn't give her another one. She scooped up Harvey, tucked him under her arm and went into the shop.

In the end shop, in amongst the glass and silver bits and pieces, she found a small porcelain model of a dog, the spitting image of Harvey, just right for Thomas's desk. She went home well pleased with her finds, and found Thomas sitting by the drawing room fire reading the papers.

'Oh, how lovely; you're home. No, don't get up. I'll tell Cork I'm back and we'll have tea.'

When she had poured the tea and offered him sandwiches she asked, 'Have you had a busy day?'

Mr Tait-Bullen bit into a buttered scone. 'Much as usual.' He offered Harvey a bit of scone, and didn't see the disappointment on her face. He seemed to shut her out of his working life sometimes. Perhaps he thought that she was not really interested. He added, 'You have created quite a sensation, you know...'

'Me? Didn't I behave like a consultant's wife? Shouldn't I have danced so much?'

'You behaved beautifully, my dear, and everyone is enchanted by you. I was inundated with invitations. I can see that we have a busy social winter ahead of us.'

'Do you mind that? If you do, I'll make excuses.'

'No, you mustn't do that. I rely on you to organise our leisure, and several of the invitations will be for you alone, I imagine—coffee mornings and tea parties.'

He finished his tea, and, with the remark that he had work to do, went to his study. Harvey went with him and she was left sitting alone. She had declared rather too quickly that she had letters to write, and he had nodded casually with the remark that they would meet at dinner.

He had told her before they married that he wanted a companion. It seemed to her that he had forgotten that— or was it that she bored him? She told herself not to be silly, allowing imagination—and, it must be admitted, a modicum of self-pity—to take over.

But she forgot all that when at dinner he suggested that they leave early on Sunday morning so that they might take a look at some likely villages not too far from Little Planting.

'Is there any particular village you fancy? We might at least look around us, so that after Christmas we can house-hunt in earnest.'

'Would we spend the weekends there?'

'Whenever possible, and any free days that I can manage. Somewhere not too far from a good road back to town.'

'Well, there's a lovely little village—Child Okeford—south of Shaftesbury, close to Blandford, and only a mile or so from the main roads. Years ago I used to go there with Mother, she had an old schoolfriend living there, but she moved away. I dare say it's changed. I must have been nine or ten years old.'

'Then we will have a look at it before we go to Little Planting. If we leave really early we should have plenty of time to look around.'

They left at eight o'clock. It still wasn't full daylight, and the streets were Sunday morning quiet. The presents were packed in the boot, and Harvey, wrapped in an old shawl, slept peacefully on the back seat. Claudia felt her spirits soar as she got into the car. She was wearing the leather jacket over a silk shirt and a tweed skirt, and leather boots which had cost so much that she felt quite faint when she thought about it. But they were worth every penny—as supple as velvet and exactly matching the colour of her jacket.

She would have liked to draw Thomas's attention to them, but he seldom noticed what she wore, although he never failed to tell her that she looked nice. But he didn't *look*, she reflected, not at her, not to see her in detail, as it were. She dismissed the thought as unworthy; he was a kind and thoughtful husband and they got on famously.

They reached Child Okeford an hour and a half later.

There was a pale watery sun now, and the village still slept under it. In another hour there would be church, and people setting off in their cars or going for a country walk, but for the moment they had the place to themselves.

'Could we park and look around?' asked Claudia.

They left the car in the centre of the village and, with Harvey on his lead, began to explore.

'It hasn't changed much,' said Claudia. 'The village shop's still there, and the pub.' They paused to admire the church and walked the length of the main street, stopping to explore the narrow side turnings. It was a charming place, its cottages well kept, with one or two bigger houses standing back from the road. They had gone its length when Claudia saw a narrow lane leading away from it, half hidden by high hedges.

'Let's take a look, Thomas...'

The lane curved, and they passed two cottages with their doors opening directly onto the lane, and then round the next curve they saw another cottage, quite large, standing behind hedges. There was a 'For Sale' board beside its old-fashioned wrought iron gate.

It must have been empty for some time, for the windows were uncurtained and the garden was woefully overgrown.

Claudia looked at Thomas, and he opened the gate and they walked up the brick path to the solid door under the thatched porch. There were windows on either side, and small windows above, tucked away under the thatch.

Claudia went to peer through one of the windows. 'The kitchen,' she said. 'There's another window at the side, and two doors. Come and look, Thomas.'

She went round the side of the cottage and found a door, and, at the back, more windows. A quite large

room and next to it a room which took up the whole of
the other side of the cottage. She bent to peer through
the letterbox. 'There's a staircase,' she told Thomas, but
when she turned round he wasn't there. He was by the
gate, writing down the address of the house agents.

'Oh, Thomas, do you like it? I mean, well enough to
want to see inside?'

Mr Tait-Bullen put away his notebook and walked up
the path to join her.

'Yes, I like it, too. The agent is a local man—
Blandford—supposing we go and see him? I'll phone
him from the car—he might even come here to us.'

'Now? This morning? Oh, Thomas…'

He looked at her, smiling a little. Her cheeks were
flushed and her eyes shone with excitement. He had the
sudden urge to wrap her in his arms and kiss her. The
thought took him by surprise; it was as though he was
seeing her for the first time.

'Now, this morning,' he assured her, and nothing in
his level voice showed his feelings.

They went back to the car and he phoned from there.
The agent was willing to drive to meet them at the cottage. He would be with them in half an hour, he assured
them.

'Shall we phone your mother?' suggested Thomas.
'Tell her that we may be a little later than we intended?'

That done, they went back to the cottage, and while
they were waiting poked round the garden. It was quite
large, and there was a rough track at the side of it which
led to a sizeable barn.

'The garage?' asked Claudia hopefully. 'And, look,
there was a greenhouse there and a summer house…'
She clutched his arm. 'Oh, Thomas.'

The agent was middle-aged and fatherly, wearing

comfortable country tweeds and carrying a bunch of large keys. When Mr Tait-Bullen apologised for disturbing his Sunday, he made light of it. 'Come inside,' he invited. 'It's solid enough, roof was thatched a couple of years ago, brick and cob walls, the usual mod cons; the old lady who lived here went into a nursing home six months ago, but she kept the place in good order.'

He opened the door with a flourish and stood aside to let them in.

The hall was narrow, with a staircase along one wall. There were three doors, and Claudia opened the first one. The room was large, with windows both at the front and the back of the house, an inglenook and open beams. Claudia rotated slowly, seeing the room in her mind's eye just how it would look—an open fire, comfortable chairs, little tables with lamps on them, bookshelves. She crossed the hall, taking Thomas with her. The room on the other side of the hall was smaller, with cupboards on either side of an old-fashioned grate and more open beams.

'The dining room,' she breathed happily, and went into the kitchen. A quite large room, with an old-fashioned dresser and windows on either side of a door to the garden. And upstairs, leading off the small landing, were three rooms, two of them small but the third of an ample size. There was a bathroom too, rather old-fashioned, but the plumbing, the agent assured them, was up-to-date.

Claudia wandered round on her own while the two men talked quietly in the hall, and presently Thomas went in search of her. She was hanging out of a bedroom window, planning the garden in her mind's eye.

'You like it? I've made an offer; he'll let me know tomorrow when he's contacted the owner.'

Claudia flung her arms round his neck. 'Thomas, oh, Thomas!' And she kissed him. She hadn't kissed him like that before, and she drew back at once, rather red in the face. 'Sorry—I got carried away.'

Mr Tait-Bullen didn't allow the normally calm expression on his face to alter. The kiss had stirred him, but all he said was, 'Let us hope that we are able to buy the place.'

She reminded herself that he was not a man to be easily aroused from his habitual calm. But he liked the little place; she could see that. They would furnish it together and spend happy weekends there and get to know each other.

CHAPTER SEVEN

CLAUDIA'S mother came to meet them as they stopped before George's door.

'Darling, what kept you? You haven't had an accident?' She looked anxiously at Thomas. 'All you said was that you were unexpectedly delayed... But come in, do, there's coffee and mince pies...'

It had been a happy day, reflected Claudia, sitting beside Thomas as he drove back to London in the early evening. Such a lot of cheerful talk, presents to exchange, Tombs and Mrs Pratt to visit, a walk after lunch with Rob and Harvey, and, of course, the cottage to be discussed while the men exchanged views on medical matters.

Claudia, with her mother's enthusiastic help had had the place metaphorically furnished, the curtains hung and the garden dug and in full bloom by the time they got into the car. She'd still been thinking about it as Thomas began the journey home.

'Blue and white checked curtains in the kitchen, and that white china with blue rings round it—you know the kind I mean?'

'I can't say that I do, but I shall leave such matters to you—if and when the cottage is ours.'

She felt a stab of disappointment. Furnishing the little place together would have been fun. She reminded herself that he was a busy man, and that any free time he had he would want to spend in a way to please himself.

She said, 'It was a lovely day, Thomas, thank you for bringing me. Harvey enjoyed himself too.'

They didn't talk much more on the way back. Thomas replied cheerfully enough to her remarks, but she sensed indifference. A polite indifference, but all the same it was there, like an invisible wall between them. It was a relief to get home and find Cork waiting for them in the warm, well lighted hall.

He led Harvey away to the kitchen for his supper, and Claudia, casting off her jacket, followed him.

'Have you had a pleasant day, Cork?'

'Yes, thank you, madam. I trust that you had an enjoyable trip?'

'Yes, yes, we did.' She would have liked to tell him about the cottage, but perhaps Thomas might not like that.

Cork, spooning Harvey's supper into a dish, said civilly, 'Would supper in half an hour suit you, madam?'

She said that yes, that would be fine, and wandered away out of the kitchen and up to her room to tidy herself. When she went downstairs presently there was no sign of Thomas.

Cork met her in the hall. 'The Professor has been called away—an emergency—he will phone you as soon as he is able. He had no time to say more, madam.'

Claudia stood in the hall looking at him, saying nothing, so he added, 'I'll serve you supper at once—there's no knowing when he will be back, madam.'

'All right, Cork. Let's hope it's nothing that will keep him away for too long.'

She ate her solitary meal and then went to sit in the drawing room, with Harvey for company. The evening was well advanced by now, and there had been no message. She sat there, pretending to read, her ears stretched to hear the sound of his return or a phone call, but there was neither. At midnight she took Harvey to his bed in the kitchen, and bade Cork goodnight after being told that he would wait up— 'The Professor wouldn't want you to lose your sleep, madam,' he said, and was interrupted by the phone.

He answered it, and then handed it to Claudia.

'Go to bed, Claudia. I shall probably be here for most of the night. Sleep well—I'll have a word with Cork.'

She handed the phone to Cork, who listened with an expressionless face. His 'Very well, sir' was uttered in a disapproving voice, and when he rang off he said, 'I am not to wait up, madam. I'll lock up as soon as you are upstairs.'

There was nothing else to do but wish him goodnight, give Harvey a quick cuddle and go to her room.

She had expected to stay awake, waiting for Thomas's return, but she fell asleep almost at once to wake hours later, not knowing why she had wakened. The house was quiet, but all the same she got up, peered at her clock and saw that it was almost four o'clock. She got into her dressing gown and slippers and crept downstairs, and as she reached the hall, the front door opened very quietly and Thomas came in.

He closed the door equally quietly before he spoke. 'Shouldn't you be in bed?'

Disappointment at his terse greeting turned her pleasure at seeing him to peevishness. 'Of course I should,' she snapped. 'I'm not in the habit of wandering round the house at this hour. I woke up—I don't know why...'

She started towards the kitchen. 'I'll get you a drink; you're tired.'

'Nothing to drink, thank you, but I am tired. Go back

to bed. I'll go to bed myself as soon as I've put my bag
away.'

She felt a childish wish to burst into tears. He was
behaving as though he wished she wasn't there. She
turned to go upstairs again, and then paused.

'At what time will you want breakfast?'

He was already at his study door. 'The usual time.'

'But it's after four o'clock!'

He didn't answer, but went in and shut the door. Now
that there was no one to see, she allowed unhappy tears
to trickle down her cheeks as she went upstairs.

As for Mr Tait-Bullen, he sat down at his desk and
allowed all kinds of thoughts to fill his head. The sight
of Claudia, standing in the hall in her pink gown, her
hair in glorious wildness with that look on her face, had
disturbed him deeply. When he had envisaged being
married to her he hadn't imagined anything like that. She
was Claudia, a girl he admired and liked, a perfect companion and a wife whose company he would enjoy without any of the hazards of being in love with her.

Being in love was something he had lost faith in years
ago, when he had given his heart to a woman and it had
been thrown back to him. Not that his heart had been
broken, not even cracked—indeed, he had remained happily heart-whole ever since. But, since then, falling in
love had been something in which he didn't believe.

And now, suddenly, he had discovered that that
wasn't true.

Claudia, crying her eyes out in the comfort of her bed,
fell asleep at last, and woke a few hours later looking
much the worse for wear. She still looked beautiful, but
her eyelids were pink and so was the tip of her delightful
nose; she disguised the pinkness with expensive cream

and powder guaranteed to work miracles, happily unaware that they made no difference at all, and went down
to breakfast, rehearsing a few polite remarks about the
weather as she went, just to let Thomas see that their
unfortunate conversation earlier that morning was to be
ignored.

He was already at the table, the post scattered around
his plate. He got up as she went to the table and wished
her good morning in a brisk voice which warned her that
he didn't wish to talk, so she discarded the weather and
replied even more briskly. Cork, offering coffee, buttered eggs and fresh toast, returned to the kitchen quite
worried, for he had allowed himself to approve of his
mistress after a doubtful start. She didn't interfere, but
at the same time she had made it her business to know
exactly how the house was run—without interfering. She
was looking unhappy, and he was uneasy.

'If it was anyone else but the Professor,' he told
Harvey, 'I'd have said it was a tiff, but he's not one to
waste his time on anything as silly. Very polite he is this
morning, too—in a rage, no doubt. And she's been crying…'

Harvey looked sympathetic and allowed his ears to
droop, so that Cork felt constrained to offer him a couple
of nicely crisped bacon rinds.

Mr Tait-Bullen studied Claudia from beneath lowered
lids; she had been crying, but it seemed best not to mention that, for she wore a haughty expression which
warned him off. It was hardly the moment to tell her
that he had fallen in love with her. Claudia, being
Claudia, would probably turn on him and tell him not to
talk nonsense.

He said mildly, 'I hope to be home for tea today.'

Claudia said, 'Very well, Thomas,' and, since she was

anxious to be friends, even though they weren't on the best of terms at the moment, added, 'Is there any shopping you need? Have we all the presents for your family?'

'If you would check the list? Have we remembered Mrs Rumbold?'

'Yes—a cardigan. Would you mind if I added a box of chocolates? A big box tied with ribbon…'

'By all means.' He got to his feet. 'I'll see you later. Enjoy your day.'

It was her last chance to find a present for Thomas. It was a pity that he had everything. She had the little figure of the dog like Harvey, but that wasn't enough. She spent an anxious morning peering into shop windows; a tie wasn't enough, besides, he might not like it—all the same she bought one in a rich silk—dark, glowing colours in a subdued pattern.

Looking at a display of photo frames gave her an idea. She chose a small one in silver and took it back home, found one of the photos which Tombs had taken at their wedding and inserted it. It wasn't a very good photo, but they had both been laughing—perhaps it would remind him that they had declared their intention of making their sensible marriage a success!

She was in the drawing room, bent over a piece of tapestry she had bought, of roses on a creamy background which, when finished, would become a cushion cover, when Thomas came home. She saw with relief that he was his usual calm self, and they had tea together, talking casually—Christmas, his work, Harvey's progress, Christmas again—and later, after dinner, they sat together in the drawing room, she with her tapestry, he with the evening papers and his medical journals. Just like an old married couple, thought Claudia contentedly.

She must remember not to bother him when he had had
a hard day.

It was almost dark when she took Harvey for his evening trot the next day. It was cold, but dry, and a brisk
run in the park would do him good. There were few
people about—most were shopping frenziedly for
Christmas. She kept to the main paths and decided to
keep Harvey on his lead. He was an obedient little beast,
but if he were frightened by something he might run off
in a panic. She had turned back towards the road when
two youths passed her, and then turned and followed her.
She didn't dare look round, but she picked up Harvey
and quickened her pace. The road wasn't more than a
few minutes' walk away, and there would be other people…

Only there weren't—there was no one in sight!

She could feel they were close to her now. Should she
run for it, scream, or turn and confront them? She spun
round and found them within inches of her.

Mr Tait-Bullen, arriving home earlier than he had expected, found the sitting room and drawing room empty.
Cork, coming to meet him in the hall, wished him good
evening, adding that Mrs Tait-Bullen had taken Harvey
for a run in Hyde Park.

'I did suggest that it was a bit dark, sir, but she said
that they both needed a breath of fresh air. She usually
goes there from the Bayswater Road.'

'Then I'll go and meet her,' said Mr Tait-Bullen, and
got into his overcoat again. 'Explain to her if she gets
back first, Cork.'

The streets were almost empty and he walked fast,
which was a good thing, for he had no sooner got to the
park than he heard Harvey's shrill bark.

It was quite dark now, but he could see Claudia and the two youths. As he reached them she landed a nicely placed kick on one of the youth's shins and he yelped with pain.

'Let's 'ave the dog and break 'is neck for him...'

Thomas didn't waste time in talk. He knocked the pair off their feet, begged them in a terrifyingly quiet voice to be off before he called the police, and turned his attention to Claudia.

The youths scrambled to their feet and ran off, and Claudia said in a rather shaky voice, 'Oh, thank you, Thomas. They were going to hurt Harvey.'

Thomas's quiet voice was harsh. 'They were going to hurt you, too. It was foolish of you to come here at this time of day; you have only yourself to blame.'

He had turned her round and was marching her back, out of the park, into the lighted respectable streets with their sedate houses and infrequent passers-by.

She hadn't expected that; she had expected sympathy, kindly concern, enquiries as to whether she had been frightened or hurt. The fact that he had only uttered the truth made no difference. Rage and delayed fright made her shiver. He was an inhuman monster! Scathing remarks she would have liked to make in reply remained unuttered, for they were walking too fast for her to talk; his hand on her arm urged her forward, but it didn't feel friendly.

Mr Tait-Bullen, aware of her thoughts, remained silent. The wish to sweep her into his arms, Harvey and all, was strong, but if he did that, and kissed her, things might get out of hand. Rather, let her dislike him for the moment than be frightened off by a love she hadn't expected or asked for.

Indoors once more, he took Harvey from her, took off

her coat and gloves, sat her down in the drawing room and put a glass in her hand.

'Drink this; it will make you feel better.' He sounded like a friendly family doctor.

'What is it?'

'Brandy. You don't like it, but drink it—there's a good girl.'

She tossed it back, caught her breath, whooped, was slapped gently on the back and burst into tears.

'I'm not crying,' said Claudia fiercely. 'It's this beastly brandy.'

He forebore from comment, only smiled a little and went away to take off his own coat. Cork was hovering in the hall. 'Madam isn't hurt? An accident?'

'Thugs. No, she isn't hurt—only frightened and shocked.'

'I'll bring in the tea at once.'

'Splendid, and give Harvey a biscuit or a bone. He's been frightened, too.'

Cork, quite shaken, glided away, to return within a few minutes with the tea tray and Harvey.

He arranged the tea things on a table convenient to Claudia, murmured his regrets at her unpleasant adventure, assured her that the crumpets were freshly toasted and took himself off. His mistress certainly didn't look quite the thing; she was usually as neat as a new pin, but now her hair was decidedly untidy and she was crying. He hoped that the master would comfort her in the proper fashion.

Claudia, in a haze of brandy, took the handkerchief which Thomas offered and mopped her face and blew her nose.

'I'll go and tidy myself,' she muttered, and started to get out of her chair.

'No need. You look very nice as you are.' Thomas's voice was soothing, and at the same time matter-of-fact. 'I'll pour the tea; the brandy will wear off if you eat something.'

He was regretting his harshness in the park; he had been afraid for her when he had first caught sight of her with the youths and fear had made him angry. He must repair the damage as quickly as possible.

He gave her tea, and put a crumpet on a plate and set it on the small table by her chair. He said cheerfully, 'You know, you had me scared for a moment—those boys can be so rough. Will you promise me not to go into the parks—any of them—once it is dusk?'

'All right—you were so angry…'

'Yes, but it was anger which spilled over from those thugs, and I had no right to blame you. Life at Little Planting is free from such unpleasant encounters—you weren't to know…'

It was going to be all right again, thought Claudia. They were back on their friendly footing once more. She bit into her crumpet. 'I should have used my head,' she conceded.

They didn't hurry over their tea; Thomas led the talk round to Christmas, and their journey north. 'There are some splendid walks,' he told her, 'and there is a special beauty in winter. I'm looking forward to showing you something of the countryside.'

'I'll bring my boots…'

'And something warm to wear. Have you had time to tie up all the presents?'

She nodded. 'Yes, and I've put in one or two extra things—some chocolates and a scarf and some scent, just in case we've missed someone out, or someone turns up who isn't expected.'

Nothing had changed, reflected Claudia, going to bed after a quiet evening with Thomas. True, he hadn't said much, but just having him there, sitting opposite her, was nice...

They were to drive up to Finsthwaite on Christmas Eve. A long drive but, as Thomas pointed out, they would be on a motorway for almost the whole distance: the M1 as far as Birmingham, then the M6 until they left it, just before Kendal, and took the road to the lower end of Lake Windermere and, a few miles further on, Finsthwaite— a matter of just under three hundred miles. He would go to the hospital in the morning, and they should be able to leave London by mid-afternoon—a little over four hours' driving; once out of town and on the motorway, it would be a straightforward run.

Claudia packed carefully, made sure that the presents were stowed in the big box Cork found for her, and collected Harvey's basket, tins of food and his favourite bone. She would travel in the leather jacket, with a tweed skirt and a cashmere sweater—suitable garments if they were to go walking. She took her winter coat, too, for she was sure they would go to church, and added a little velvet hat, one of the jersey dresses, the green patterned dress, silk shirts and cardigans, sensible shoes—her boots she would wear—and a pair of elegant slippers. She wanted Thomas to be proud of her...

They left at three o'clock. The afternoon was already turning into a raw, cold evening, but the shops were lighted, there were Christmas trees and coloured lights and, as they drove out of the city, pavements packed with last-minute shoppers.

'I love Christmas,' said Claudia happily. 'And people look so happy... I hope Cork will have a good time.'

'I fancy he will. His widowed sister comes for Christmas Day, and on Boxing Day some old friends of his come to lunch and stay until the evening.'

'Oh, good.'

She stayed silent then, while he threaded his way through the streets until they were on the M1.

'We'll stop this side of Birmingham for a cup of tea and allow Harvey a breath of air. There's a service station.'

After that he was mostly silent, but it was a friendly silence, and Claudia had a good deal to think about. His family—she had met his parents, but only briefly at the wedding. Supposing his mother had decided that she didn't like her? And his sisters... She began to compose a series of suitable topics of conversation.

The Rolls swept with silent speed towards Birmingham. There wasn't much traffic going north, and nothing impeded its progress. The service station lights loomed ahead of them and they parked and got out, glad of a few minutes to stretch their legs while Harvey aired his tail and then, tucked under Claudia's arm, went with them to the restaurant.

Thomas found a table, told her to sit down and went away to fetch their tea. Watching him coming back, with a tray of tea things and a plate of buttered teacakes, Claudia thought that Cork would have a fit if he could see his master now.

They didn't waste time, but drank the strong hot tea, ate the teacakes and, since there was no one to see for the moment, Claudia gave Harvey a saucer of milk, tucked a paper napkin under his small chin and fed him the last of the teacakes.

'Are we going to stop again?' she asked.

'If necessary. I'd like to get off the motorway before we do, but if you need to stop say so.'

'I was thinking of Harvey,' said Claudia primly.

Mr Tait-Bullen suppressed a chuckle. 'Of course. But with luck he'll sleep for a few hours.'

They were bypassing Liverpool in just over an hour; in another hour they were off the motorway and through Kendal. There the road was still good, but narrow in places, with long stretches of dark countryside and few villages—Grigghall, Croathwaite, Bowland Bridge, and then nothing until they rounded the end of the lake at Staveley. Now the road had become a narrow lane, running between trees.

Finsthwaite was a small village: farms, a cluster of cottages, a village store and post office, the church, and a village school lower down a gentle slope. A short walk away there was Grizedale Forest. It was a little paradise, but now shrouded in darkness, save for a few lighted windows, and then, unexpectedly, a lighted Christmas tree by the church.

Thomas drove through the village, turned into an open gateway and stopped before the house where he had been born; it was a nice old house, built of grey stone, with light streaming from its windows and its solid door flung open before they were out of the car.

Claudia need not have worried about her welcome. She was drawn at once into the family circle, kissed and hugged, helped out of her coat, then carried away by Ann and Amy to warm herself by the log fire in the drawing room and be plied with delicious coffee.

'Just to warm you up,' said Ann. 'Dinner will be in about half an hour. Don't change.' She hesitated. 'Well, perhaps you'd rather. Did you have a good trip here?

Thomas is such a good driver. A pity it was dark, but I don't suppose you could come any earlier?'

When Claudia had finished her coffee they took her up the wide staircase at the back of the hall and along the gallery above it. 'You're here, Thomas's dressing room is next to it, and there's a bathroom. I expect he'll be up presently. Come down as soon as you can; we've still got to put the presents round the tree.'

They left her then, in the high-ceilinged big room. The furniture was big too: a vast brass bed, a tallboy and a mighty wardrobe in mahogany, and an old-fashioned dressing table with a great many little drawers and a triple mirror standing in the window. Despite the heavy furniture the room was charming, with its sprigged wallpaper, thick cream carpet and chintz curtains and bed-cover, and two bedside tables, each with a rose-shaded lamp.

Claudia opened the door in the further wall and saw the bathroom beyond, and another door on its opposite side which she opened too. The dressing room.

She went back then, unpacked her case, which some-one had brought to the room, and changed into the patterned jersey. She did her hair and her face and then sat down on the bed. She was suddenly nervous of going downstairs. Thomas had no right to leave her alone...

There was a tap on the door and Thomas came in. He took one look at her and sat down beside her on the bed. 'Feeling a bit overpowered?' he asked, and put an arm round her shoulders. 'Don't—they are all so delighted to see you. Come down; Father's waiting to open the champagne and James wants to kiss you under the mistletoe!'

They went down to the drawing room together, and Claudia stifled a wish that Thomas had been the one who wanted to kiss her. A silly wish, she reflected. He wasn't a demonstrative man... Hadn't he told her that before they married? That he had no interest in being in love, that he had loved once, but never again? And she had accepted that.

Everyone was in the drawing room—a square room with two windows overlooking the front garden. It had panelled walls, and chairs that were roomy and very slightly shabby, but the furniture was solid and beautifully kept, the chairs covered in a dark red damask which matched the curtains, and a vast sofa before the stone fireplace, which housed a roaring log fire. The room was warm—warm with content and happiness and love; there was no doubting the affection Thomas's family had for each other, although it wasn't on display.

They drank their champagne and presently crossed the hall to the dining room. It was panelled, like the drawing room, and had a vast mahogany table surrounded by Victorian balloon back chairs, a William the Fourth pedestal sideboard, which took up almost all of one wall, and a magnificent giltwood side table. There were a number of paintings on the walls—Claudia supposed that they were family portraits—dimly lit by wall sconces.

The table had been decked for Christmas, with a centrepiece of holly and Christmas roses, a white damask cloth and napkins, and heavy silverware. When the soup was served Claudia recognised Coalport china.

She was hungry and dinner was excellent: game soup, roast pheasant and a chocolate and almond pudding. She wasn't sure what she was drinking; all she knew was that she was very happy and enjoying herself. And Thomas, sitting beside her, had once or twice put his hand over hers, which gave her a warm glow inside.

They arranged the presents round the tree after dinner.

'We all go to church in the morning,' Amy told her. 'But perhaps you and Thomas would like to go to the midnight service? It's only a short walk to the church and it's a lovely service. We always went, but now we have the children we stay at home. They still wake in the night sometimes, and we like to be there.'

'How many have you?'

'Two, and another one in the spring. Ann has one so far.' She smiled. 'They're such fun, but an awful lot of work.'

Claudia went to sit by her mother-in-law then, until that lady declared that it was time they all went to bed. 'You still have the children's stockings to fill,' she reminded them. 'Breakfast at eight o'clock. Church at half-ten.'

'I'm taking Claudia to the midnight service,' said Thomas quietly, and smiled across the room at her.

'Then we'll leave the side door unlocked. I'll tell Maggie to leave coffee on the Aga, and there are sandwiches in the fridge if you feel hungry.'

There was a leisurely round of goodnights as the party broke up, leaving Claudia and Thomas sitting by the fire.

'Well?' he asked. 'Are you going to like my family?'

'Yes, very much. I've never had more than Mother—and Father, of course, but he died several years ago. I think it must be wonderful to be one of a large family.'

'Indeed, it is. We don't see a great deal of each other, but we make a point of meeting for important occasions. Amy and Ann are happily married—Jake and Will are sound men—and I suppose James will marry in due course.'

'Your mother and father aren't lonely so far from you all?'

'No. They are happy to be together. Mother has her garden, Father sits on various committees, and they both enjoy walking. Besides, there is quite a social life here, even in the winter.'

He glanced at the walnut long case clock. 'Would you like to walk to church? It's only a question of five or ten minutes.'

'I'll go and get a coat.'

It would be cold outside. She put on her winter coat and the little velvet hat, found gloves and sensible shoes, and went back downstairs to where Thomas was waiting for her in the hall.

He took her to a door beyond the staircase and opened it onto the night. There was a clear sky, alight with stars and a dying moon, and he walked her along a path leading from the side door of the house to a small gate which led onto the lane.

'The church is below the village,' he told her, and took her arm. And round a bend she saw its squat tower close by. There were other people making their way there, too, and when they reached the church she saw that it was already almost full. Thomas made his unhurried way to a pew in the front, stopping to greet people he knew and introduce her, but presently she had time to glance around her. The church was small, rather cold, but scented with the evergreens and holly and Christmas flowers which decorated it. She liked it, and she enjoyed the service, simple and peaceful.

They walked home later, and Claudia said, 'It's Christmas Day…'

Thomas stopped. 'Ah, yes, and we have no need to wait for the mistletoe.' He hugged her close and kissed her, and then let her go rather abruptly. He had very nearly lost his self-control.

Claudia had enjoyed the kiss very much; if she hadn't been taken by surprise she would have kissed him back, but he had released her before she had the chance. Perhaps later…

The house was in darkness as they went quietly through the side door and into the kitchen. It was a thoroughly old-fashioned one, with a huge dresser along one wall, a big scrubbed table with ash and elm Windsor chairs around it, and two elbow chairs on either side of the Aga. The floor was of flagstones and there was a rag rug before the Aga. Harvey was fast asleep in his basket, and curled up on one of the chairs was a large tabby cat.

Thomas fetched two mugs and poured their coffee. 'Maggie has been with us for a lifetime,' he told her. 'She's a really marvellous cook. We all love her, and the children can't be kept away from her when they come to stay. She has plenty of help, of course, but both maids have gone home for Christmas Eve. They'll be here in the morning, and go again after lunch. There's an ancient man who does the heavy work in the garden; he should have been pensioned off years ago, but the people round here don't retire.'

'Would you rather live here than in London?'

'This is my home, and I love it, but my work is in London and that is my life. I am fortunate enough to be able to have both.' He glanced at her. 'You like living in London, Claudia?'

'Oh, yes, you have a lovely home, and the parks are close by.'

'I've bought the cottage at Child Okeford. We'll go down to see it in the New Year. It seems pretty sound, but it will need painting and some small alterations.'

'You've bought it? Oh, Thomas, how splendid. Did you forget to tell me?'

'I didn't know myself until this morning, when the agent phoned. You're pleased?'

'Yes. Oh, yes. You're pleased, too?'

'Yes!' He got up and took her mug. 'It's very late. Go to bed, my dear, you have had a long day.'

'And a very happy one.' She leaned up and kissed his cheek. 'This is such a lovely Christmas.'

For a second time that evening Thomas very nearly lost his self-imposed restraint.

Claudia went down to breakfast in the morning to a chorus of greetings and good wishes. The children were there too. Ann's small son was in a high chair, but Amy's two—little girls—were sitting at table. There was a lot of noise and laughing while they ate, and afterwards, before they all went to church.

Claudia could see that Thomas was on excellent terms with his nephew and nieces. He would be a splendid father, only it seemed that he had no desire to be one. Perhaps in a few years' time, when they had grown closer to each other... She shut the thought away; he had married her for companionship and because he wanted a wife to order his household and entertain his friends. Their marriage was a sensible one, based on friendship and compatibility, and a genuine liking for each other.

The church was warmer now, and there were even more people there. She stood between Thomas and his mother and sang the carols, and told herself that she was the luckiest girl on earth.

CHAPTER EIGHT

CHRISTMAS dinner was at midday, so that the children could share it—turkey and Brussels sprouts, roasted potatoes, braised celery, cranberry sauce—nothing had been overlooked. Then the Christmas pudding, set alight with great ceremony, and last of all mince pies. They drank champagne again, and then coffee before going to the drawing room to open their presents. The children first, of course, before they went for their afternoon naps, and for a while the room was awash with coloured paper, ribbon and toys.

Presently it was the grown-ups' turn. Everyone was there, including Maggie, the two maids and the gardener, and they collected their gifts first, drank a glass of sherry and went off to the kitchen to enjoy a splendid high tea.

Mr Tait-Bullen Senior handed out the presents, and very soon the room was just as untidy as when the children had been there. Claudia, looking round her, thought how delightful the room looked, with the lighted tree and the gaily covered presents, the roaring fire and the soft lamplight. She wished that her mother and George could have been there, too, although when she had phoned her mother that morning that lady had sounded in the best of good spirits. She caught Thomas's eye and smiled—a wobbly smile, for she was on the verge of tears—and he came to sit by her, taking her hand in his large, cool one and giving it a friendly squeeze.

'You haven't opened all your presents…'

'No. There are so many and they're all so lovely.' She

picked up a small box and tore away the paper. A jeweller's box, blue velvet and quite small. She looked at the tag then, and said, 'Oh, Thomas, it's from you....' She opened it and looked at the earrings bedded in white satin—sapphires in a network of gold and diamonds.

'Oh, Thomas...'

'Go on, kiss him,' said Amy, who had been watching. 'You're in the family now.' They had all turned to look, smiling and nodding, so she kissed him, very pink in the cheeks, feeling shy.

Thomas didn't kiss her back. She thought he might have done, with everyone watching, but he took the earrings out of the box and fitted the hooks neatly into her ears. She got up then, and went to admire the earrings in the gilt mirror opposite the fireplace, and that gave her time to let the blush die down and regain her composure.

She still had more presents to open, so she went back and sat down again on the massive sofa beside Thomas and started to open them. A gorgeous silk scarf from Harvey, who was sitting at her feet and muttered sleepily when she thanked him. A leather writing case from her in-laws—red leather with her initials. Gloves and scent and a jewel case from Thomas's sisters and brother. She went round thanking everyone, and being thanked, and when she sat down again Thomas was opening his presents. He had a great many, but he saved hers till the last, quietly approving of the tie. When he unwrapped the photo frame he said nothing for a few moments.

'It's a kind of reminder,' said Claudia quickly. Perhaps he didn't like it; perhaps he thought it was a silly, sentimental thing to have done.

'I shall put it on my desk at my consulting room,' he

told her quietly, 'so that everyone can see what a beautiful wife I have.'

'That wasn't why I did it,' she told him. 'I thought it would remind you...' She paused to get it right. 'It's difficult to explain...'

'Then don't try, Claudia. I think I understand and I shall treasure it.'

The presents had all been opened by now, and everyone was sitting round, content to do nothing for the moment.

'Shall we go for a quick walk?' Thomas pulled her to her feet.

'Yes, dear, take Claudia towards the forest,' his mother said. 'Tea will be a little later because of the children. Be back by five o'clock.'

So Claudia fetched her coat, tied her new scarf over her head, got into her boots and went down to the hall where Thomas, coated but bare-headed, was waiting.

They went out of the side door again, and along the lane towards the church, and then turned away along a rough track which took them almost at once into the forest. It was a perfect late afternoon, the sky in the west a blaze of red and yellow, the rest of the heavens already darkening, lights from the village and outlying farms twinkling.

'It's been such a lovely day,' said Claudia as they walked along arm in arm. 'I feel happy, don't you, Thomas?'

He didn't answer that, but observed, 'It would be hard to be unhappy here. Some places are meant to be happy in—I think the cottage at Child Okeford will be such a place.' He looked down at her face, rosy with the cold. 'What are we going to call it?'

'Why, Christmas Cottage, of course.' She went on

happily. 'We'll have a cat—at least, he'll have to live with us in London and go to and fro like Harvey... Should we have brought Harvey out with us?'

'Harvey is sleeping off a much too large dinner. I'll give him a run after tea.'

'Your parents haven't got a dog? I know Maggie has a cat...'

'Jasper, our Labrador, died a month or so ago. He was old and a devoted friend. In a while, when they are over his death, I've arranged for a puppy—another Labrador—to join the family.'

'Oh, Thomas, how kind. They must miss him terribly.' She stopped to stare into his face in the gathering dusk. 'You think of everything, don't you?'

'I do my best.' He reflected that he hadn't thought of falling in love...

They walked back presently, to eat Christmas cake and drink tea from delicate porcelain tea cups round the fire while the children sat at a small table eating an early supper. They had had an exciting day and were inclined to be peevish. Amy and Claudia went to sit with them, coaxing them to eat their peanut butter sandwiches, the little fairy cakes Maggie had made for them, which followed the Marmite toast, and to drink their milk.

When they were borne off to bed there were plaintive requests for Daddy to tuck them up and read them a story. They were taken upstairs then, and presently Amy and Ann came down again. 'Now it's your turn,' Amy told the men, and as they went away she said laughingly to Thomas, 'Just you wait; it'll be your turn next. I don't know why fathers read bedtime stories better than mothers, but be prepared for it!'

Thomas said mildly, 'What do you suggest? That I start re-reading Hans Anderson? A bit out of date, I dare say. How about the *Wind in the Willows*? My favourite when I was a small boy.'

The conversation became general then, and Claudia joined in, avoiding Thomas's eye. She supposed that there would be a good many such remarks, but, since they didn't seem to disconcert Thomas, she must learn to treat them in a light-hearted manner.

She had married him so quickly there hadn't been time to foresee the small pitfalls, but as long as he didn't mind, she wouldn't allow it to bother her.

Everyone went away to dress presently, and when she came downstairs there were guests, invited for a drink— local people who, it seemed, had known Thomas and his family for years. They accepted her as one of the family at once, but the talk inevitably turned to reminiscences, so that she felt an outsider despite everyone's efforts to include her in their talk. But she did her best, and Thomas's hand on her arm reassured her.

When the last guest had gone, they went in to supper. A buffet—the vast sideboard laden with bowls and dishes filled with Maggie's delicious food: smoked salmon, salads of every kind, a ham on the bone, stuffed eggs, chicken pie, miniature hot rolls. Claudia allowed Thomas to fill her plate and found herself sitting by James.

'Pity you have to go back tomorrow. I suppose Thomas can't be away for more than a few days. Time he took a holiday. He doesn't need to work quite so hard, you know.'

'Yes, I do know, but he loves his work, doesn't he? It's important to him.'

'He's good, of course, you know that. You should see him in Theatre...'

'And people like him, I think. He came to see my

great-uncle, you know—that's how we met...' She paused, remembering that she hadn't much liked him then. 'They got on awfully well together. People do things for him, too, don't they?'

James chuckled. 'Well, he can be a bit hoity-toity if he can't get what he wants—in the nicest possible way, mind you. And in no time they are all doing exactly what he wants!'

But it was something Ann said which made her vaguely uneasy.

'You're so right for Thomas. We've all hoped he would marry, but for years and years—ever since he had that miserable love affair with that girl who went off with a tycoon from South America—he's been considered a splendid catch. Not that he's bothered about that. I don't suppose you've met a woman called Honor Thompson? She'll be livid when she hears that he's married...'

'I've met her,' said Claudia in a carefully level voice.

'You have? I expect Thomas told you about her. She's one of the persistent ones. Don't let her worry you, though. He doesn't care tuppence for any of them. He's always known what he wanted from life and now he's got you.'

Was that why Thomas had married her? she wondered. To be a barrier against wishful partners? Someone who wouldn't spoil the even tenor of his life by demanding undying love? Really, it was a sound idea! An undemanding relationship, the tolerance of good friends towards each other, shared pleasures—and they did like the same things. He could have married Honor, or any other of his women acquaintances if he had wished, but he had chosen her. Well, she was quite prepared to be the wife he wanted. And just let Honor try any of her tricks, Claudia thought waspishly.

They didn't leave until after lunch on the following day. In the morning they had gone for another walk, taking one of the paths which led into the heart of the forest. They had talked about Christmas, and plans to come again, perhaps for Easter, or perhaps he could persuade his parents to visit them.

'The cottage should be quite ready by then, and I'm sure they would enjoy it. We will go down there as soon as possible and see what needs doing. I'm sure you have some ideas, and the place will need painting and decorating.'

'And furnishing.' Claudia's eyes sparkled. 'Curtains and things.'

It had been a most satisfactory morning, she reflected, and began a leisurely round of goodbyes. Christmas had been two wonderful days; she liked Thomas's family, and she loved the countryside around his home and the comfortable old house. She hoped that they would come again, but she doubted if Thomas could spare the time to drive up frequently. She got into the car with real regret, made sure that Harvey was comfortable on his blanket on the back seat, and turned to give a final wave.

It was still light, although the day was fading. She looked around her at the country as Thomas drove back to join the motorway, and, since he didn't speak other than to ask her if she was comfortable, she stayed silent.

They were approaching the motorway when he said, 'We'll stop for tea just before Birmingham, but do tell me if you want to stop before then.'

Her, 'Yes, Thomas,' was the epitome of wifely obedience.

It was quite some time before he said, 'You're very quiet?'

'Well, I thought that's what you wanted. I'm sure you have a great deal to think about...'

'For instance?' He sounded amused.

'Your work and your patients, and perhaps you are wishing you were back with your family and that Christmas was just beginning and not over.'

He didn't comment on that. 'You enjoyed your Christmas?'

'Oh, I did. I loved every minute of it, and I like your parents and your sisters and brother.'

'They like you, Claudia.'

They stopped for tea at a service station, took Harvey for a brisk walk around the car park and resumed their journey, speeding along the motorway, talking of this and that. And Claudia had the feeling that even while he talked Thomas's mind was on something else.

'Are you worried about something?' she asked. 'You don't have to talk if you don't want to. I shan't take umbrage.'

He laughed then. 'I'm not worried, Claudia.' He began to talk about plans for Christmas Cottage, and she felt as though she had been snubbed. It had been nicely done, but whatever it was, she wasn't to be told about it.

London was empty of traffic; Boxing Day was a family visiting day and many people were indoors. Later they would return to their own homes, but just now it was quiet.

Cork opened the door and they went in to a welcoming warmth and a faint but delicious smell from the kitchen. He welcomed them with grave pleasure, fetched the cases and then announced that dinner would be in half an hour if that suited them.

'Excellent,' said Thomas. 'I'll take Harvey for a run.' Which left Claudia to go to her room and tidy herself and unpack before going down to the drawing room. Thomas wasn't there, but Harvey was sitting before the fire looking drowsy.

'I gave Harvey his supper, madam,' said Cork, coming silently into the room. 'The master's in his study; he will be joining you presently.'

'Thank you, Cork. Have you had a happy Christmas?'

'Very pleasant, madam. I trust that you enjoyed yourself?'

'Very much. The country was beautiful.'

Cork went away, and she fetched her tapestry and began to stitch. It was a bit of an anticlimax after the cheerful racket that had been such fun. Only yesterday, she thought, and it seems like weeks ago already.

Mr Tait-Bullen, coming into the drawing room some minutes later, paused for a moment in the doorway; Claudia looked delightful, sitting there working away at her embroidery. It seemed to him that she had always been there; it was hard to think of the house without her in it. He wondered what she would say if he were to tell her that he had fallen in love with her, but he thrust the temptation aside. He thought she was happy and content, and he must have patience; in time she might come to love him, but until then they must stay good friends. It was lucky that he had more than enough work to keep him busy.

He sat down opposite her and observed mildly, 'I've a good deal of work on my hands for the next week or so, but we might go down to Child Okeford next Sunday and take a good look round. You might like to spend an hour or two with your mother.'

'Yes, I would, and I'm longing to see the cottage again. You don't have to go away, do you?'

'In a couple of weeks I have a seminar in Liverpool— two days or so.' He gave her a thoughtful look. 'I'm afraid you will be on your own a good deal, Claudia.'

'Oh, I don't mind that,' she said cheerfully. 'I've all those coffee mornings and tea parties to go to—with people I met at the hospital ball—and plans for the cottage.'

'Ah, yes. You must decide how you want it furnished…'

'Well, you must decide too, for you'll be living there as well, whenever we get the chance.'

They spent the rest of the evening together. 'Like an old married couple,' said Cork to himself. 'They ought to be out dancing or whatever. It isn't right.'

Such an idea hadn't entered Claudia's head. She was perfectly content, sitting there, making heavy weather of the tapestry while Thomas immersed himself in a pile of medical journals. It was nice, she reflected, that they enjoyed each other's company but made no demands on each other.

Soon after ten o'clock she folded her work, declared that she was tired and took herself off to bed, after giving Harvey a hug and bestowing a friendly goodnight on Thomas as he got up to open the door for her. His manners were beautiful, she reflected as she went upstairs, and he was unfailingly kind. She heaved a sigh, not knowing quite why.

She didn't see a great deal of him for the next few days. He was away early in the mornings and didn't get home until early evening; there was a good deal of flu, he told her, and his registrar was off sick.

'Take care!' said Claudia. 'Are there many off sick at the hospital?'

'Amongst the nursing staff, yes—quite a few of the medical staff, too. And, of course, the wards are all full…'

There was nothing she could do to help, but she took care to see that a meal was ready when he got home, with welcoming warmth and no disturbances if he wanted to work. As for herself, her days were nicely filled. Walks with Harvey, such shopping as Cork allowed her to do, coffee with various of the ladies she had met at the ball and most afternoons spent reading though not always understanding some of the medical books in Thomas's study. But it was necessary that she had some idea of his work, and now was no time to bother him with any questions. If ever he chose to talk to her about work, at least she would have some idea of what he was talking about.

There was also the New Year to look forward to— only a day away—and all being well they were to go out to dinner tonight, and dance the New Year in. Claudia washed her hair, did her nails and massaged in a cream guaranteed to improve the complexion. That she had no need of it was quite beside the point.

She took Harvey for a long walk in the afternoon and returned home, thankful to be out of the damp cold, looking forward to tea round the fire. She let herself in, dried Harvey and took off her outdoor things, then went to sit down in the small sitting room. It was already past the usual teatime, but she supposed that Cork had forgotten the time. After half an hour she went to the

kitchen, vaguely uneasy. Cork ran the house like clock-
work. Perhaps he had had to go out for some reason…

He was huddled in a chair by the Aga, with a white
face and shivering.

'Cork, you're ill.' She put a hand on his forehead and
felt its heat. 'You must go to bed at once.' When he
protested feebly, she added, 'No, please do as I say.'
She saw that the effort to get out of the chair was too
much for him, so she heaved him up and helped him to
his room, sat him on the bed, took off his shoes and
pulled the bedclothes over him. 'Now, lie still, there's a
good man. I'm going to get you a drink.'

There was bottled water in the fridge; she filled a jug,
found a glass and took them to his room, gave him a
drink and tucked the bedclothes round him.

'Your tea, madam,' croaked Cork. He closed his eyes.

'Don't give it a thought. Go to sleep if you can. I'm
going to find a warm water bottle for you. As soon as
the Professor gets home he'll come and see you. I expect
it's the flu.' She cast a worried glance at him. He really
looked ill; thank heaven Thomas would be home early.

She went to the kitchen and made a pot of tea. Cork
wouldn't have any, although he drank some more of the
water, so she went back to the kitchen and drank her
own tea. She ate some of the sandwiches on the tray,
fed Harvey, and, since they wouldn't be going out to
spend the evening, peered into the fridge and the cupboards, collecting the makings of a meal.

She was still there when Thomas came home. Harvey
ran into the hall to greet him, and as the dog came into
the kitchen, with Thomas behind him, she dropped the
potato she was peeling and ran to him, quite forgetting
to be calm and sensible.

'Thomas, I'm so glad to see you. Cork's ill. I've put

him to bed but he's so hot and shivery.' She tugged at his sleeve. 'Do come and see what's wrong.'

Mr Tait-Bullen's features displayed nothing but calm assurance. He said in an unhurried manner, 'This wretched flu, I expect. I'll take a look.' He paused on his way. 'You didn't take his temperature?'

'Well, no. His teeth were chattering so much I was afraid he would break the thermometer.'

He nodded and went out of the kitchen and into Cork's room, and Claudia peeled the last of the potatoes. There was plenty of food in the fridge; she had chosen salmon steaks to go with the potatoes, frozen petit pois and there was a cabbage in the sink to clean and cook. Dull fare for Old Year's Night, but with Cork ill, food didn't seem very important.

'It will have to be cheese and biscuits afterwards,' she told Harvey, 'and I just hope he likes it.'

'He'll like it,' said Thomas, from somewhere behind her. 'Cork has the flu, but he's not too bad. I've given him paracetamol and I'll go back presently and settle him down. We've plenty of orange juice and cold drinks, I presume? That's all he'll need for a while...'

'Poor man. Now, just you sit down and I'll make a pot of tea. Supper won't be very exciting, but it'll be food...'

Mr Tait-Bullen sat, watching his wife trot to and fro, her glorious hair getting very untidy, her lovely face flushed. She might look a bit disorganised, he reflected, but she was efficient and quick. A pot of tea was placed before him, with the sandwiches, now rather dry, and a dish of the little cakes Cork was so clever at baking.

'If you don't mind waiting for dinner, I'll go and see to Cork.'

'My dear girl, he would rather die. He needs to be undressed and put to bed—washed and so on.'

'Oh, well, I'm quite able to do that, you know.'

'Of course you are. All the same, I think it is better if I see to him while you get our dinner. By all means see to his drinks and any food that may take his fancy.'

He got to his feet. 'I'll check the post and be back very shortly.'

He was as good as his word. 'We'll eat here, shall we?' he asked, taking off his jacket. 'I'll see to the table presently.' He didn't wait for an answer, but went to Cork's room and shut the door.

Claudia drank another cup of cooling tea, offered Harvey a biscuit, because he was being such a good boy, and turned her attention to the salmon. She was a good cook; if she had known that she was to cook the meal that evening she would have thought out a dinner worthy of the occasion, but it would have to be a simple meal. She thought with regret of the pretty dress she had laid out ready to wear this evening, the delicious supper they would have had, the excitement of toasting the New Year. What could they have for a pudding? she wondered, and began to squeeze oranges for poor Cork.

Thomas came back presently, put on his jacket and then started to lay the table. It took some time, since he had to search for everything in drawers and cupboards, but the end result was as elegant as if Cork had done it himself. He took a bowl of hyacinths from the window-sill and put it at the centre of the table, arranged silver and glass just so, and went to look in the fridge. Cork, that admirable man, had put a couple of bottles of champagne in it earlier that day. Thomas opened one, filled a glass and took it to Claudia.

'I'm sorry—you must be disappointed that we can't

go dining and dancing with the rest of the world,' he told her. 'We'll make up for it later on.'

Claudia took a good drink of champagne. 'I don't mind a bit; I'm so sorry for Cork.' She wrinkled her nose. 'Why does champagne make you feel so uplifted?'

'A good question.' He topped up her glass. 'Something smells good.'

Claudia drained the cabbage, chopped it fine, added nutmeg and a squeeze of lemon and put it on the dish Thomas had got from the dresser. She had creamed the potatoes with plenty of butter and milk and dished up the peas; now she laid the salmon on two warmed plates and took it to the table.

'Not very exciting, I'm afraid,' she said. 'But there's a nice piece of Stilton for pudding!'

Mr Tait-Bullen, who had snatched a sandwich for his lunch, cleared the plate. 'You're a good cook,' he told her. 'What a treasure I have married.'

Claudia went pink. 'Well, I can't cook anything fancy. Great-Uncle William didn't hold with spending a great deal of money on what he called "elaborate food" so I became good at fancying up sausages and things.'

'Tell me more about your great-uncle,' suggested Thomas and filled her glass again.

And Claudia, nothing loath, her tongue nicely loosened by the champagne, told—until she stopped suddenly. 'I'm being boring. It's all the champagne—you should have stopped me...'

Mr Tait-Bullen, enjoying himself, made haste to assure her that he hadn't been in the least bored. 'After all, we know very little about each other even now.'

While she made coffee he went to look at Cork.

'Sleeping like a baby. Now, let us discuss the cottage. As soon as Cork is better, we will spend a day at Child

Okeford, see what is to be done and get hold of a builder.
We had better find a gardener too, to get the place into
some shape before we can take over. I'll get hold of the
estate agent—he may be able to recommend someone.
We will try not to alter the place too much, but the barn
will need a secure door and a firm run-in for the car.
Had you thought of anything you wanted changed or
added to?'

Claudia shook her head. 'I loved it as it was. Will it
take long, the necessary repairs and the garden?'

'It shouldn't do. We can choose carpets and furniture
once we have all the measurements. A local firm, I think,
don't you? Sherborne or Shaftesbury.'

'Carpets and curtains,' said Claudia happily, 'and
comfortable furniture. Thomas, it will cost an awful lot
of money…'

'Probably, but it will be our second home, won't it?
We mustn't spoil the ship for ha'porth of tar.'

They washed the dishes together then, and in no time
at all, it seemed, it was five minutes to midnight.

Cork was still asleep. Thomas came back into the
kitchen, filled their glasses and went to stand by her. As
the clock struck midnight they toasted the New Year,
and then he took the glass from her hand, put it with his
on the table and bent to kiss her. An unhurried, gentle
kiss, quite different from his usual rather brisk salute, it
stirred something inside Claudia's person, and she stared
up into his face, vaguely puzzled.

He was as calm as he always was. 'A Happy New
Year, my dear.'

'You too, Thomas.' She paused. 'You're quite happy,
aren't you? I mean, with us being married? We're good
friends, aren't we? And I promise I'll not get in your

way—with your work, you know. When we married I hadn't thought of all the things which could go wrong.'

He had seen the puzzled look; his Sleeping Beauty was beginning to wake up. He said in a matter-of-fact manner, 'I'm very happy, Claudia. Getting married was something I should have done years ago—to you, of course!'

'Well, you didn't know me, did you? Do you have to go to the hospital tomorrow—no, today?'

'No, unless I'm needed. Supposing we go down to the cottage?'

'But we can't leave Cork.'

He took the phone out of his pocket and dialled.

'A male nurse will be along at eight o'clock; he'll stay with Cork until we get back. He's a good man—kind and trustworthy.'

'But won't he be on duty?'

'No, he has days off, and he'll be glad of the fee.'

'Oh, won't anyone mind?'

He smiled and shook his head, and she said, 'Are you so important that you can do things like that?'

'I must admit to having a certain amount of clout.'

'Well, it would be marvellous. All day? We must take a notebook and pen and a tape measure. But only if Cork feels better…'

'Of course. Now, go to bed, Claudia. If we're to leave early you'll need your beauty sleep.' He added, 'You don't need any beauty sleep, actually. You're already as beautiful as it is possible to be.'

A remark so unlike Thomas that she stopped to stare at him. Then, 'It's all that champagne,' she told him. 'You're looking at me through rose-coloured spectacles.'

Thomas only smiled, and he didn't kiss her as she went past him. She was quite disappointed.

Mr Tait-Bullen saw to Cork, locked up and took himself off to his study. He still had reports to read, patients' notes to examine, his workload to be checked. Harvey went with him, to snooze on his shoes until Thomas went to his bed after a last visit to Cork, who, while still very much under the weather, was prepared to stay alive after all.

Claudia woke soon after six o'clock and went down to the kitchen to make tea. She peeped at Cork, made him another jug of lemonade, laid the table and went back to dress. A day at the cottage meant sensible clothes: the leather jacket, a sensible tweed skirt and a pullover. She made short work of her hair, did almost nothing to her face, and went back downstairs. She could hear the murmur of voices from Cork's room as she set about frying bacon and eggs and making toast, and presently Thomas came in with a short, middle-aged man.

He wished her good morning and added, 'This is Sam Peverell, my dear. Sam, my wife. We'll have breakfast as soon as it's ready. You know what to do for Cork, and you can reach me on my mobile, of course, if you need me. We should be back in the early evening.'

Claudia piled plates with bacon and eggs and made more toast. 'I'll put your lunch ready for you, Mr Peverell, and a tray for tea. There are oranges and lemons in the fridge, and milk and yoghurt. So will you help yourself?'

'Certainly, Mrs Tait-Bullen.' He turned to Thomas. 'Phone calls, sir?'

'I'll put on the answering machine. But get hold of someone at the hospital if you're worried.'

'It's very kind of you to come, Mr Peverell,' said Claudia. 'On your day off, too. We're awfully grateful.'

'No problem, Mrs Tait-Bullen. My wife's gone to her

mother's, and the girls are spending the day with friends.'

'You have daughters?'

'Two, fourteen and sixteen, and you wouldn't believe what a worry they are...'

Mr Tait-Bullen sat back, listening to Claudia charming Sam—a martinet on the ward, a splendid nurse and reputed not to have much of an opinion of young women. *His* Claudia, he reminded himself, who was a delight to the eye and the ear and whom he loved.

They left well before nine o'clock, and, since the streets were almost empty after the night's celebrations, they were on the motorway in no time at all. They stopped at a service station after more than an hour's driving, had coffee and allowed Harvey a brief stroll before resuming their journey. Claudia felt a little thrill of excitement as Thomas turned the Rolls into the network of small lanes which would lead them to Child Okeford. Supposing they didn't like the cottage now that they had the leisure to look it over?

'Where's the key?' asked Claudia, a bit late in the day.

'I'm to fetch it from the end cottage as we pass.'

The village was quiet, its inhabitants no doubt sleeping off the excesses of the previous night, but when Thomas knocked on the cottage door he was soon given the key; several keys, in fact.

The cottage looked a bit forlorn, for it was a dull morning with the hint of rain, but Claudia, seeing it in her mind's eye with roses round the door, curtains at the open windows, the garden full of flowers, skipped inside the moment Thomas had the door open.

They went slowly from room to room, checking them with the particulars which the estate agent had sent. The cottage was in good heart, its small windows secure and solid, large cupboards, the stairs sound. The kitchen would need cupboards and shelves, and an Aga, and its flagstone floor cleaned, but the vast stone sink was something Claudia wanted to keep.

They went round a second time while Claudia argued the merits of porridge-coloured carpeting against different colours in each room. Thomas listened patiently, told her to have whatever she liked and suggested that they went and looked round the garden. It was larger than they had first thought, and there were apple trees forming a screen between the garden and the open fields beyond.

'We can grow vegetables,' said Claudia, quite carried away, 'and there's space for a little greenhouse, and we could have a small summer house in that corner, so that you could have somewhere quiet to go.'

Thomas agreed gravely, waiting to see if she would suggest a swimming pool, but she didn't. She did suggest a rockery, and a little pool where frogs might live.

They went to the village pub presently, and ate a ploughman's lunch and emptied a pot of coffee between them. The cottage was every bit as delightful as they remembered it—better, even, for now they had explored it from bottom to roof.

'I'll get on to the agent tomorrow,' said Thomas, 'and get things started.'

He glanced at his watch. 'Do you want to see your mother and George as we go back?'

'May I? Is there time? And what about Cork?'

'I'll check when we go back to the cottage. We must lock up properly.'

Claudia beamed at him across the pub table. 'Oh, Thomas, I'm so happy...'

CHAPTER NINE

CLAUDIA'S glow of happiness lasted until they were back home. They had called at George's house, had tea with him and her mother, and stayed for a while. Claudia and her mother had a lot to say to each other, but, mindful of Cork, she'd got up at once when Thomas suggested mildly that they should go. It wasn't for a while that she'd realised Thomas was rather silent. She'd stopped talking then, sitting quietly beside him, still happy, her thoughts busily occupied with the cottage.

It wasn't until they were home again, and Sam Peverell had given his report, pocketed his fee and gone home, and she had been to see Cork and gone to the kitchen to get a meal, that she realised that Thomas, after seeing Sam Peverell off home and spending a short time with Cork, had gone to his study and shut the door.

It was as if he had erected an invisible barrier between them. She told herself that he was probably tired or had work to do, and that the faint air of reserve would have disappeared by the time their supper was ready.

Lamb chops, sprouts, potatoes and mint sauce. Plain fare indeed, but it was already after seven o'clock and she still had to cook... She rummaged around in the cupboards, found what she wanted, made an apple pie and popped it in the oven and then made an egg custard for Cork. He was feeling more himself, assuring her that he would be on his feet in another day or so, adding,

164

with a touch of suspicion, that he hoped she could find everything she wanted in the kitchen.

'Oh, indeed I could, Cork, and I've been careful to put everything back where it belongs.' She gave him a motherly smile. 'We do miss your lovely cooking.'

Cork, still pale and poorly, nevertheless looked smug at that.

The first few days of January went swiftly by; Claudia enjoyed them, for she was kept busy shopping and cooking, and although Mrs Rumbold came each day there was always something to be done: the flowers to arrange, the phone to answer, bills to pay. She was careful to ask Cork's advice about most things, and in a few days, when he was feeling better, he sat by the Aga, warmly wrapped, and advised her about the best methods to cook their meals.

She found this rather tiresome, since she was a capable cook, but she knew that he meant it kindly and nothing would have induced her to snub him. And Cork, for his part, acknowledged the fact that she was an ideal mistress, never encroaching on his preserves while asserting a gentle authority. The master was a lucky man.

The master was a busy man too, away early in the morning and for the most part not back again until the early evening. He made time, though, to visit Cork, and spent what leisure he had in Claudia's company, although she sensed his reserve towards her. She tried to remember if she had said or done something to annoy him and wondered if she had disappointed him in some way. One day, she promised herself, when he wasn't away from home so much, she would ask him.

Cork, back on his feet once more, took over his normal duties again. He made her a little speech of thanks with the voice and manner of a benevolent person, making it quite clear that, much though he had appreciated her help, he no longer required it. Claudia, thrown back onto her own resources, took long walks with Harvey, drank coffee with various of the wives she had met at the ball, and ploughed her way through the books in Thomas's study, not understanding them by half but feeling that by doing so she was bridging the gap which she felt was between them.

It was something of a relief when he told her that he had to go to Liverpool for two or three days, and would she like to visit her mother?

'I can drop you off on my way, and then why not bring your mother back here for a day or so? There's the possibility that I may go on to Leeds and have to spend the night there.'

'I'd like that, Thomas. I'll phone Mother; I'm sure she'd love to come, and we might do some shopping.'

'Yes, well, take her to Harrods or Harvey Nichols and use our account.'

He looked so kind when he said it that she was tempted to ask him if there was anything wrong, but she didn't; he had come home later than usual and he looked tired.

Harvey was to stay with Cork, for she intended to stay only one night at George's house; she and her mother could return by train and they would spend two days together. Her mother hadn't seen Thomas's home, and Claudia was longing to show it to her. They could have a good gossip and shop. She got into the car two days later, on a still dark morning, and Thomas drove out of town, leaving Cork and a protesting Harvey behind.

'I hope Harvey won't pine,' said Claudia, 'and that

Cork will take care of himself…all alone,' she added doubtfully.

'I should imagine that he is pleased to see the back of us. He now has the opportunity to take a nap when he feels like it, and rearrange everything around the house to his satisfaction. He will spoil Harvey, bully Mrs Rumbold, and probably drink my port.'

She laughed. 'He'd never do that; he's your devoted slave.'

'And yours, I fancy. I'll phone you this evening, but don't worry if you don't hear from me after that. I'll let you know when I'm coming home.'

They didn't talk much, just casual remarks from time to time, and although Thomas was friendly it was as though the real Thomas was hidden behind this pleasant man sitting beside her. She could say something about that now, she supposed, but then changed her mind. He wouldn't want to be bothered when he had the seminar ahead of him to think about.

They reached George's house by mid-morning and, despite her mother's pleas that he should stay for lunch, he was on his way again after a cup of coffee. Claudia went with him to the car and he kissed her lightly as he got in. She poked her head through the window as he was about to drive off.

'Do be careful, Thomas, and I hope everything is successful.'

Her face was very close to his, and he drew back with a jerk, an action which sent a cold shiver down her spine. She stood back, fighting sudden tears. It was as though he couldn't bear her near him. When he got home again they would have to talk…

She enjoyed her day with her mother and George.

That they were quietly happy together was evident, and Mrs Pratt and Tombs were, in their own way, just as happy. George drove them over to Child Okeford one evening, and they looked round the cottage. She hadn't got the key, but the builders had already started on the repairs and they peered through the windows and explored the garden. George pronounced it a nice little property, and her mother could find no fault with it.

She bore her mother off to London the next day. Thomas had phoned on the previous evening, expressed the hope that she was enjoying herself and warned her that he might not phone her for a couple of days. He had sounded friendly, but even over the telephone she'd imagined she could hear the constraint in his voice.

Her mother was delighted with the London house. She professed herself overwhelmed with its comfort and luxury, and Cork's perfections. Claudia took her walking in the park with Harvey, and the next day went shopping with her. George had given her money with which to buy herself something she liked, and Claudia, mindful of Thomas's suggestion, persuaded her mother to accept a cashmere twinset, and the wool skirt which went so well with it...

Thomas had told her not to expect to hear from him for a day or so, but all the same she was disappointed that there was no word from him. She had to explain this to her mother, who said roundly, 'The poor man; it's time he slowed down. After all, he's a married man now; his work is important, but so is his married life.'

Claudia said cheerfully, 'He loves his work, Mother, but once the cottage is ready we shall be able to spend weekends there, away from his patients.'

She took her mother to the station the following morning and saw her onto the train. Feeling suddenly lonely, Claudia lingered at the station entrance, trying to decide whether she would join the taxi queue or walk home. She could cross the road and go through Hyde Park—quite a long walk, but it would fill in her morning.

She had left the park, crossed Park Lane and was walking along Brook Street when she came face to face with Honor.

She summoned a social smile and a hello, and went on walking, but Honor put out a hand so that she was forced to stop.

'Claudia—it is Claudia, isn't it? How delightful to meet you again. I've been away; I can't stand London at this time of year. I phoned Thomas at his rooms before I left, and he told me that you were very occupied getting ready for Christmas. Such a bore, having to go all that way to the Lakes just for a couple of days.'

'I enjoyed it,' said Claudia. 'Nice to see you again. I really must get on…'

Honor didn't let go of her arm. 'My dear, you can spare half an hour, surely? Let's have a cup of coffee…?'

Against her will, Claudia agreed. Perhaps Honor really was an old friend of Thomas's, in which case she shouldn't be rude—besides, Honor was making herself pleasant.

Over coffee, after a witty account of her holiday in Italy, Honor began asking questions put so casually it was difficult to ignore them.

'Thomas is away?' she asked. 'Off on one of his jaunts?'

'Well, it's not a jaunt. He's in Liverpool, and probably going on to Leeds.'

'Has he taken Emma with him?' Honor gave Claudia a sly glance. 'His secretary goes everywhere with him. A beautiful creature—very efficient and very sexy. Of course, now he's a married man, I expect he's more discreet.'

'I haven't the least idea what you're talking about.'

Honor said quickly, 'Oh, my dear, I'm sorry. I quite thought you knew. After all, it isn't as if you and Thomas are desperately in love—anyone could see with their eyes that neither of you are...' She paused as Claudia got to her feet.

'You're talking rubbish, and spiteful rubbish at that,' said Claudia. 'If making mischief is all you know how to do, I pity you.'

'You're upset,' said Honor. 'Naturally. You don't have to believe me, but if you ring Thomas's rooms I'm quite sure that Emma won't be there.'

'I'll do no such thing,' said Claudia. 'Goodbye, Honor, I hope we don't need to meet again.'

Honor had a parting shot. 'You wouldn't dare find out for yourself,' she laughed. 'But I shouldn't be surprised to hear that Thomas won't be home for a few more days.'

Claudia didn't answer that, but walked out of the elegant café where they had been sitting and then walked all the way home.

This gave her time to remember every word Honor had said, and to assure herself over and over again that nothing would induce her to phone his rooms—a nasty, low-down action not to be contemplated.

She hardly touched the lunch Cork had ready for her; she took Harvey for his afternoon walk, and the moment she got back picked up the phone.

Mrs Truelove answered. After an exchange of pleasantries, she said that, no, Emma wasn't there. 'She doesn't come in when the Professor is on one of his trips. A most efficient girl,' enthused Mrs Truelove, 'quite indispensable.'

Claudia chatted for a few minutes before putting down the phone. Mrs Truelove hadn't asked her why she had rung, and she hoped that she wouldn't wonder about it later. She felt mean and wicked and disloyal, but no more so than Thomas...

'I hate him,' said Claudia to Harvey, and burst into tears. She didn't hate him, she loved him, and what a time to discover it.

Before she'd made that shattering discovery it wouldn't have mattered about Emma—after all, he had never said that he loved her or was likely to do so. Theirs was to be a sensible marriage, wasn't it? So he was free to do what he liked, wasn't he? She knew that he would never be unkind to her, would always be a friend, even be a little fond of her and share at least some of her life, but now, with the discovery that she loved him, that wouldn't do.

This was something they would have to talk about. She would never tell him that she had fallen in love with him, but she would make sure that he wasn't having second thoughts about their marriage. And he would be home the next day.

She had pecked at her dinner and was poking her needle in and out of her tapestry when Thomas phoned. He would be delayed for another day, perhaps two, he told her. 'I'm in Leeds; I'll come home as soon as possible.'

She said, 'Yes, Thomas. Goodnight,' and hung up on

him. If she had said more she would have burst into tears.

The next day seemed endless. She filled it with walks and arranging the flowers and trying to eat the delicious little meals Cork had set before her, but by the evening she was restless, and at ten o'clock she decided to go to bed. The day had been long enough, and there was all tomorrow to get through before Thomas got home.

'Bed,' she told Harvey, and started towards the kitchen with him, but in the hall he stopped and rushed to the door, barking furiously, and a moment later Thomas came in.

He closed the door gently behind him, bent to fondle Harvey and looked at Claudia, standing speechless. She had rehearsed all the things she was going to say to him but she couldn't remember a word of them. She said, 'Hello,' and then, 'You said you'd be home tomorrow.'

'I'm home today because something's wrong, isn't it? You were upset when I phoned last night.'

He was taking off his coat as he spoke, and Cork, coming into the hall, greeted him with grave pleasure, took the coat, enquired if he would like a meal or drinks and then went away, taking Harvey with him.

'Cut the air with a knife, I could,' Cork told the little dog. 'What's up, I'd like to know. Well, we'll have to leave them to it, won't we? And hope it comes out in the wash.'

Harvey, accepting a biscuit, wagged his ridiculous tail.

Claudia found her voice. 'Would you like a meal, or something to drink?'

Thomas smiled briefly. 'Cork just asked me; you couldn't have been listening. And, no, I don't need anything. What I do need is to know why you sounded as you did last evening?'

Claudia, playing for time, asked, 'How did I sound?'

'Don't waste time, Claudia. You were upset, angry—too angry to speak to me. Why?'

He took her by the arm, marched her into the drawing room and shut the door. 'Let us sit down...'

He sounded friendly, and reassuringly calm, and she longed to fling herself at him, feel his arms around her, but first she must know about this secretary of his. She wouldn't mention Honor, for he might dismiss her as a malicious gossip bent on making mischief, and perhaps she was, but Mrs Truelove was quite another kettle of fish.

'Where do you go when you aren't at a hospital? I mean, do you have friends or stay at a hotel—in the evenings when you're free.'

If she had been looking at him she would have seen the sudden stern set of his mouth and his cool stare, but she wasn't, so she plunged on, getting muddled and resenting his calm silence. 'Don't you meet people you know? Or—or have a meal out, or something?'

She did look up then, and sat up straight at the sight of his cold anger.

He said in a quiet, icy voice, 'Are you accusing me of something, Claudia? Perhaps you should be more explicit.'

She had gone too far now to stop. Besides, she had to know... She steeled herself to look at his expressionless face. 'Your secretary, Emma—she wasn't at your rooms. Mrs Truelove said that she was never there when you were away...'

Mr Tait-Bullen crossed one long leg over the other.

He said mildly, 'You wish to know where she was for some reason?'

'Yes, well, I think you should have been honest about it. I know it doesn't matter, because we—we don't love each other, but I am your wife.'

'Let me get this quite clear. You have been told by someone that when I go away Emma goes with me, so when I'm not working we can—er—live it up together.'

He spoke quietly, but Claudia flinched at the contempt in his voice. 'And who told you this?' He smiled thinly. 'I'll give you credit for not imagining it for yourself.'

'Of course I didn't imagine it,' said Claudia hotly. 'It never entered my head. I met Honor...'

'And you believed her?'

She peeped at his face. He was in a splendid rage, but he was controlling it with an iron will. She said recklessly now, knowing that she had cooked her goose with a vengeance, 'Not quite. I tried not to think about what she had said, but she told me Emma wasn't at your rooms—she laughed and said I didn't dare to find out for myself... So I did. I phoned Mrs Truelove and she told me that Emma wasn't there.'

'I see.' He got to his feet. 'Our marriage may not be quite as other marriages, Claudia, but I thought that we shared a mutual trust, and I hoped that our liking might have turned into something deeper in time. It seems as if I was wrong. This is something which must be put right as soon as possible. If you are unhappy, and I think you are, you must make up your mind what you want to do. Take your time, and we'll talk again later.'

He walked to the door. 'And now I must do some work. Goodnight, Claudia.'

She said in a squeaky voice, 'Thomas, are you very angry?'

He smiled then. 'Yes, my dear.' It was a bitter smile.

She heard him whistle to Harvey and then shut his study door, and she went up to her room, reflecting that he still hadn't told her if Emma had been with him.

The night seemed endless, and by the end of it she hadn't had a single sensible thought. She would never be able to tell Thomas that she loved him now. Not that she would have done, she contradicted herself, but they would have made something of their marriage, because loving him, even secretly, would have made it worthwhile. Something would have to be done, but she had no idea what.

She went down to breakfast, her pale face carefully made up. It didn't conceal her puffy eyelids or her pinkened nose, and Thomas, bidding her good morning in his usual voice, had difficulty in restraining himself from picking her out of her chair and carrying her off somewhere quiet, where he could tell her how much he loved her. But of course that wasn't possible; she had demonstrated only too clearly last night that her feeling for him wasn't strong enough to overcome her doubts.

He said in his usual calm way, 'I shall be away all day. Could dinner be a little later? I've a meeting at the hospital, and I'm not sure how long it may last.'

He finished his breakfast, wished her a pleasant day and went away, leaving her to feed Harvey with her neglected toast.

She was trying to decide what to do when the phone rang, and she went to answer it.

'Mrs Tait-Bullen? This is Emma, the Professor's secretary. Mrs Truelove told me that you had asked for me.

I'm sorry I wasn't here; when the Professor goes away he allows me to go home—I live in Norfolk—at least, my parents do. I'm getting married in the summer, and there's such a lot of planning to do; was there something I could do for you?'

Claudia, astonished at herself, heard her own voice saying the first thing which came into her head. 'Emma, how nice of you to phone. I just wondered if you had any ideas about a wedding present? I've seen some lovely china... The Professor says I should make it a surprise, but perhaps there's something you would like to choose? A dinner set, or something for the house? Will you think about it and let me know?'

She rang off presently, Emma's thanks ringing in her ears. But she forgot that immediately. What a fool she had been; with her stupid outburst yesterday evening she had destroyed any chance of Thomas ever falling in love with her. He must despise her. They would have to go on living together, outwardly friendly, while she ate her heart out for him, and he would treat her with a distant courtesy which would chill her to the bone.

She suddenly couldn't bear it any longer. Thomas would be at his consulting rooms until ten o'clock; she picked up the phone and dialled.

Mrs Truelove answered her. The Professor had just seen a patient. If Mrs Tait-Bullen would wait a second, she would get him to come to the phone before she ushered in the next one. She came back to the phone very quickly.

'I'm so sorry, the Professor asked me to say that he is unable to talk to you at the moment. I was also to tell you that he would be late home this evening and that you weren't to wait up for him.'

The dear soul sounded worried, and Claudia hastened to say that it wasn't important and that she had expected him not to be home early. 'It was nothing important,' she added, 'really, it wasn't.' As though repeating it would convince her, as well as Mrs Truelove.

Her normal common sense had been taken over by a kind of recklessness. To stay quietly at home waiting for his return and then probably be met by his cold stare and refusal to talk was impossible. She swept upstairs, changed into a tweed skirt, a sweater and the leather jacket, pulled on boots, found scarf, gloves and a handbag and went in search of Cork.

'I'd like to go for a drive in the Mini,' she told him. 'Would you fetch it round from the garage for me, Cork, while I take Harvey for a quick walk?'

Cork put down the silver he was polishing. The Mini lived in the garage in the mews behind the house, for his use and as a second car if it was needed. It was kept in good order, ready for the road at a moment's notice, and there was no reason why Claudia shouldn't drive it. All the same, he felt doubtful.

'I could drive you, madam. The traffic's very heavy...'

'I've been driving for years,' Claudia told him, which wasn't true; she had used Great-Uncle William's old car from time to time, driving him to friends, before he took to his bed, and her mother to the nearest supermarket, but now fright and rage and bitter unhappiness had made her pot valiant. 'I won't take Harvey. I've had a message to say that the Professor won't be back until very late this evening, so something on a tray will suit me. I'll be out to lunch.'

She fastened Harvey's lead, gave Cork a reassuring

smile and went for a brisk walk, going over in her mind the route she must take to get her onto the motorway. It was still early, and the morning rush was at its height, but it was coming into the city; traffic going out of it would be much lighter.

When she got back Cork had the Mini at the door. He was still uneasy, but he received Harvey, begged her to take care as she drove away and went indoors. He wasn't a man to say much, but he voiced his doubts to Mrs Rumbold.

'Don't you worry, Mr Cork,' said that lady comfortably. 'You just said she'd had a message about him not being home early. Like as not she told him where she was going.'

Cork took comfort from that. At least Claudia had looked confident as she had driven away.

She might have looked confident, but several times during the next hour she wished herself anywhere but behind the wheel of the Mini. She was a good driver, but London traffic was something she hadn't had to deal with, and it was daunting. Only the despairing urge to get away from Thomas as far as possible kept her going.

She followed the route Thomas had taken, driving steadily, thankful at last to turn into the country roads from the motorway. It was after midday when she turned the little car from Child Okeford's main street and down the lane to Christmas Cottage.

The dry morning had clouded over, and it was drizzling. The cottage looked forlorn, although she could hear voices from within. She got out of the car and opened the front door.

There were several men working there and she stood, forgetful of her worries for a moment, marvelling at the amount of work which had been done. The walls were plastered and the woodwork painted, and two men were laying an oak floor in the sitting room.

She wished them good afternoon, told them who she was and asked if she would be in the way if she looked round.

No one minded, and one of the men led her from room to room, pointing out what had been done and what was still needed.

The plumbing was done, he pointed out, but none of the bathroom fitments had arrived yet. 'Nor yet the stuff your husband ordered for the kitchen.'

'You've been so quick....'

'Well, seeing as how there's not much work around at this time of year, and us being paid on the nail, we got started right away. Staying in the village, are you, missus?' She crossed her fingers and fibbed. 'No, I just came down to have a look on the way to visit my mother. I expect my husband and I will be coming down at the weekend if he's free.'

'Busy man, isn't he? The house agent told us he is a famous doctor.'

'Yes, he is.' She couldn't bear to think of Thomas. 'Look, I'm going to the pub for lunch, and then I want to look round the village. What time do you go?'

'We'll pack up as soon as the flooring's down—can't do much outside with this rain. About three o'clock, I should say.'

'Well, if I'm not back before you go, thank you for letting me see round. I've a key, but you'll lock up, won't you? The car won't be in the way if I leave it there? I'd like to have a walk.'

'Right you are, missus.'

They parted the best of friends, and Claudia went back to the village main street and went into the pub. It was almost two o'clock, but the landlord found coffee and sandwiches for her and, when she told him who she was, came and sat at the table while she ate, giving her a friendly insight into the village and the people who lived there. By the time she had finished her leisurely meal it was already dusk, and almost three o'clock.

She made her way back to the cottage and found the men loading their van, ready to leave. It was obvious they expected her to leave too, so she got into the Mini, reversed it into the lane so that the van could pass and waved them on. She stayed where she was, though, until they had been gone for a few minutes, then drove back and parked the car at the side of the cottage, found the key and went in.

The electricity had been turned on, but there was only one naked bulb in the kitchen. Someone had left an old wooden chair there and she sat down. Her sudden spurt of recklessness had worn itself out. She had been a fool to come, but she had wanted to see the place where she had hoped that they were going to be happy. She hadn't thought beyond that. 'I'll sit here for a bit,' she said out loud, 'and presently I'll drive back. Perhaps Thomas will let me explain.'

Mr Tait-Bullen saw the last of his private patients out, got into his car and went to the hospital, where he had a clinic and ward round waiting for him. He would be finished by teatime, and then he would go home and he and Claudia could talk. There was a great deal to be talked about. Their sensible marriage wasn't working out; after only a few short weeks she had let him see that she didn't trust him. All the same, he was going to tell her that he loved her…

The ward round went smoothly, and the clinic wasn't quite as busy as usual. He saw his new patients, giving them his meticulous attention, and then, waiting for the first of his old patients, he phoned Cork.

'Is Mrs Tait-Bullen home, Cork?'

'Sir—a good thing you called. I was getting that worried. She took the Mini early this morning, and said she wouldn't be back for lunch. Didn't say where she was going.'

'Took the Mini? Did she seem upset, Cork?'

'Worked up, as it were, sir. Left Harvey with me, said you wouldn't be home until late, and that she'd have something on a tray.'

'I see, Cork. I'll be home as soon as I can. She may have decided to go and see her mother. Phone Mrs Willis, will you, and find out? Don't ring me here as I shall leave as soon as I can.'

He put the phone down, deliberately dismissing Claudia from his mind while he looked through the patients' notes to see if there was anyone whom he should see. There wasn't; he could safely leave them to the registrar.

It was too early for the evening rush hour, and he took short cuts.

Cork was hovering in the hall when he went in, and said at once, 'She's not at Mrs Willis's. I shouldn't have let her go.'

Thomas gave him a reassuring pat on the shoulder. 'Nonsense, Cork. You weren't to know that she would be gone for so long. Besides, I think I know where she is.'

Cork brightened. 'You do, sir? I'll get your tea...'

'Later, Cork. I'll bring her back in the car. The Mini can be fetched later.'

Mr Tait-Bullen drove out of London a good deal faster than Claudia had done, and once on the motorway put his large, well-shod foot down, sliding past traffic, a sleek, dark shadow, there one minute, miles away the next. He had taken time to go to Claudia's room before he left the house, and had seen with satisfaction that she had taken no clothes with her. Indeed, all the usual things a girl would put carefully into her handbag before a day out were strewn on the dressing table. Her driving licence was there too. He had smiled when he saw it. His Claudia had left the house without her usual common sense.

He was forced to slow down once he left the motorway; all the same he made the journey in record time. He slid the car slowly up the lane and its lights showed him the Mini. He turned off his own lights and got out of the car, and saw the faint glow of light from the kitchen. He had brought Harvey with him; now he tucked the little beast under one arm, one hand over his muzzle to muffle his bark, and went into the house.

Claudia was still on the wooden chair. She was sitting very untidily and she was fast asleep, her head at an awkward angle. She would be stiff and cramped when she woke.

He stood looking at her, loving her very much, and Harvey, suddenly realising who it was sitting there, gave a small, pleased yelp. Claudia opened her eyes.

She stared up at Thomas for a few moments, eased her stiff neck away from the chair and said in a wondering voice, 'Thomas, dear Thomas. I thought I'd never see you again.'

He put Harvey down then, and stooped and swept her into his arms. He was tired, and he had been very worried, but now that didn't matter. He said slowly, 'You said "dear Thomas"...'

'Well, you are. Only I didn't know, and now it's all such an awful muddle...'

'No, it's not, my darling. You see, I love you. I've loved you for quite a while now. Just when I have despaired of you ever loving me, you called me dear Thomas.'

'Oh, you are, you are. I must have been blind or something. I think I've loved you for a long time too, only we both thought the other one didn't, didn't we?'

Mr Tait-Bullen listened to this muddled speech with delight. 'Dear love, you couldn't have put it more clearly.'

He bent and kissed her in a way which proved how right she was. 'Were you running away?' he asked, and bent to kiss her again. 'Because if you try to do so again, remember to take your driving licence with you.'

'I'll never do it again, Thomas. Thomas, you do love me? Really love me?'

'My dearest love, I would not wish to live without you.'

Claudia kissed him. 'We have the rest of our lives together,' she said, 'and we'll come here whenever we can, won't we? And be happy together—with Harvey, of course.'

'And a handful of sons and daughters, my darling. Harvey will need young company...'

'He has us.'

'Yes, and I have you too, Claudia.'

She peered up into his face. The bland calm wasn't there any more; she saw the man she loved, the man who had been there all the time.

'We're going home now,' said Mr Tait-Bullen.

Harlequin Romance®

Experience the ultimate desert fantasy with this thrilling new Sheikh miniseries!

Four best-loved Harlequin Romance® authors bring you strong, proud Arabian men, exotic eastern settings and plenty of tender passion under the hot desert sun....

Look out for:

His Desert Rose by Liz Fielding
(#3618) in August 2000

To Marry a Sheikh by Day Leclaire
(#3623) in October 2000

The Sheikh's Bride by Sophie Weston
(#3630) in November 2000

The Sheikh's Reward by Lucy Gordon
(#3634) in December 2000

Available in August, September, October and November wherever Harlequin Books are sold.

has a brand-new look!

Still offering favorite authors such as
**Muriel Jensen, Judy Christenberry,
Tina Leonard** and **Cathy Gillen Thacker.**

Look for
Harlequin AMERICAN *Romance*
at your favorite retail outlet in November 2000.

Visit us at www.eHarlequin.com

HARNEW00

HARLEQUIN

Duets™

Pick up a Harlequin Duets™ from August–October 2000 and receive $1.00 off the original cover price. *

Experience the "lighter side of love" in a Harlequin Duets™. This unbeatable value just became irresistible with our special introductory price of $4.99 U.S./$5.99 CAN. for 2 Brand-New, Full-Length Romantic Comedies.

Visit us at www.eHarlequin.com   HDMKD

You're not going to believe this offer!

In October and November 2000, buy any two Harlequin or Silhouette books and save $10.00 off future purchases, or buy any three and save $20.00 off future purchases!

Just fill out this form and attach 2 proofs of purchase (cash register receipts) from October and November 2000 books and Harlequin will send you a coupon booklet worth a total savings of $10.00 off future purchases of Harlequin and Silhouette books in 2001. Send us 3 proofs of purchase and we will send you a coupon booklet worth a total savings of $20.00 off future purchases.

Saving money has never been this easy.

I accept your offer! Please send me a coupon booklet:

Name: _____

Address: _____ City: _____

State/Prov.: _____ Zip/Postal Code: _____

Presenting...

HARLEQUIN®

REGENCY ROMANCE

Experience the opulence of the era
captured vividly in these novels. Visit elegant
country manors, town houses and the English
countryside and explore the whirlwind of
social engagements that London "Society"
revolved around. Embark on captivating
adventures with the feisty heroines who
unintentionally tame the roguish
heroes with their wit, zest
and feminine charm!

Available in October at your favorite retail outlet:

A MOST EXCEPTIONAL QUEST by Sarah Westleigh
DEAR LADY DISDAIN by Paula Marshall
SERENA by Sylvia Andrew
SCANDAL AND MISS SMITH by Julia Byrne

Look for more marriage & mayhem coming in March 2001.

HARLEQUIN®
Makes any time special ™